Officer on Deck

Cdr Sudarshan Ghosh (Retd.)

PRABHAT PAPERBACKS

Published by
PRABHAT PAPERBACKS
An imprint of Prabhat Prakashan Pvt. Ltd.
4/19 Asaf Ali Road,
New Delhi-110002 (India)
e-mail: prabhatbooks@gmail.com

ISBN 978-93-90900-22-0
OFFICER ON DECK
by Cdr Sudarshan Ghosh (Retd.)

Edition
First, 2022

Price
₹ 250.00 (Rupees Two Hundred Fifty only)

Printed at
R-Tech Offset Printers, Delhi

Officer on Deck

Dedicated to my parents, who always encouraged creativity and independent thinking

Preface

The Sun, sea, and sand...these conjure up the magic of beaches world over. Whether for a suntan, or lolling under a sand-covered mound, or even a child's carefully built sandcastle– they probably all fulfil humankind's quest for the innate evolutionary link with the marine world. After all, even the five-hundred-million-year-old tiny marine worm-like ***Ikaria wariootia*** is related to us !

But what of seafarers from times of yore? Numerous ships at sea have throughout history plied the vast oceans and seas– a few of whom not even reaching their destinations. And like all matters human, bad eggs abound in intent and execution, to stop trade routes, commit piracy or be part of a nation's military strategy. The Navies were thus born, and along with came the personnel, who 'man', operate, and maintain the vital vessels entrusted to the white-uniformed forces.

The Navy has always had its share of daring Captains (Kanhoji Angre, Napolean, and Nelson easily come to mind). It has also had a few unusual personalities, who by no means lack the required seamanship or dynamic qualities, but are the central characters for memorable events which, are bound to evoke chuckles upon reminiscing.

The fifty two odd real anecdotes in this book include more than a few such quirky individuals and stranger actual events. I have followed some simple rules in selecting the list—they were both personal experiences of naval officers and the Navy or involve the watery world. Names have been kept in initials only and some additional embellishment done at certain points in the narration.

If the book enables the lay reader to comprehend the mariners' tribulations, sometimes zany sense of humour and culture, it will be a job well done, I dare say.

Acknowledgements

I owe a whole lot of gratitude to all Naval personnel senior and junior, whose association so richly influenced my life and personal growth.

I am also very grateful for the rich contribution of my course-mates. Out of these, two tales stand out . While the one has been a experience of an ace Naval aviator pilot, the other is a nugget from a veteran Captain of a capital Ship.

My sincere thanks to my family, who held my hands throughout the whole process, over the long nights and 'weird' day routine of typing in the words. Their constant positive strokes and advice kept me going and overcoming the proverbial 'writer's block'.

Introduction

The book's title *Officer on Deck* refers to the Officer of the Day (in harbour) and Officer of the Watch (while at sea), for the Indian Navy; it also includes the Officer of the Deck (OOD) onboard US Navy and Coast Gaurd vessels.

The Officer on Deck is the direct representative of the warship or submarine's Commanding Officer , and is responsible for the Naval vessel. OOD needs to manage and handle the whole gamut of onboard activities. These include both events involving the Ship's crew , and those wherein non-Ship personnel also board the Ship. A cocktail evening hosted by the Captain, dousing a galley fire, or even occasionally resolving conflicts between Ship staff members—you name it—the OOD is the person for it.

At sea, the OOD/OOW is the keeper of Ship's navigation and safety at all times during the Watch. Assisted by the Quartermaster at the Ship's Wheel and the lookouts on the Bridge wings or Bridgetop, the OOW also reports important events or any untoward incidents to the Captain as per the latter's Standing Orders. Bar the Captain, the OOW is more or less Master of all he or she surveys over and under the vast oceanic expanses.

This book *Officer on Deck* is covered under 5 sections. Section 1 includes foibles and faux pas during swimming and pool jumping classes, and the eternal friendly rivalry between the Navy, Army and Air Force at the Tri-Services training Academy. Leading onto Section 2, the action shifts to experiential comedy (sometimes of errors) onboard the Cadets' Training Ship and during Midshipmen tenures. Included in Section 3 are a plethora of events during the year-long Technical Courses for Sub Lts .of the Executive branch; and a few during Watch- keeping time onboard Fleet ships of the Navy. The reader would be in the front seat here—to witness the touch-and-go happenstances and rambunctious mischief of youthful men in white, at study, and play. The Holi dance incident is an unforgettable one here, which brings back reminiscences of years long ago. Section 4 goes underwater right inside the innards of a submarine. The original men under 'quarantine', with Captains of diverse personalities—their trials and tribulations with retrospective laughs galore are an ode to the extremely sensitive and risk-prone environment of this most Silent Service. The last Section 5 takes the roller-coaster ride to its peak, within the hallowed corridors of Naval HQ. It supplies an eclectic mix of events, most of which involve (surprise, surprise) terrestrial fauna. But then, that fits into the concept of a Naval shore unit being referred to as a 'stone frigate'.

There is this true tale of a Naval officer's wife believing that only the sailor staffs go to sea while officers with their briefcases operate from shore-based offices. The literal logic seems okay, but when she realised her husband was absent from home and hearth for days–well, the bell rang aloud. No wonder–'all in the same boat' and 'all at sea' stress on the universal.

The full Deck of 52 tales based on actual events are quasi-memoirs mixed on the warm and cold currents of experience, luck and the instinctive bonding of mariners.

Enjoy!

Contents

Section-3

Section-4

Section-5

Section-1

RIP OFF!

We were in the Fourth Term at the Training Academy, no longer junior, and also not the senior-most, but somewhere about the middle. One dreaded test was the mandatory jump from the 7m diving board. The test involved standing at the edge of the board, and jumping feet first in the water below with an arrow-straight body. It was a Catch 22 situation, wherein without a successful jump, one could not advance to the next Term, even if one excelled in academics and other extracurricular activities. In fact, there were a few cadets in our Term, who had been relegated from our senior terms due to the jump clause.

The Term was getting on, and most of us had cleared the Jump Test, but for the few struggling stragglers, it still seemed a herculean task. Cadet N, who was a top-notch in academics, and could teach the professors a thing or two about Mathematics, was specifically anxious.

We were in an early morning swimming class well into the second half of our Term, and the swimming instructor directed N to straightaway climb the 7m board. The rest of us meanwhile were all in the swimming pool, practising our breaststrokes for the 50 metres Swimming Test, which was to be conducted later that day. N gingerly made his way up to the two storey high concrete diving board, with the rest of us sincerely praying for his success.

N shuffled along to the edge of the 7m diving board, and we could see the tension writ large on his face. "Cadet, *seedha khada raho*[1]", shouted the Instructor from below. As N straightened up with his arms flush along the sides of his upper body, we waited with bated breath for his final step into the air.

"Cadet, jump", came the Instructor's order, followed by the standard blow on the whistle. N jumped to glory but hit the water slightly askew with his legs separated into a scissor-like angle. The rest of us looked hopefully towards the Instructor and we could see him scribbling in his famous Record Sheet, which of course meant that N had finally cracked the Test because otherwise he would have been asked to go back up for a second jump.

But there was to be a twist in the tale for N on that fateful day.

N kept swimming around in the pool for the rest of the period, with the rest of us back-slapping him. Relief was evident on his face, especially since the path for his advancement to the next Term was now more or less clear. The whistle blow for the end of the period sounded, and we rapidly exited the pool for the quick shower and to dress up for the next class in the Academic block. However, it seemed that N was loath to leave the pool; slowly swimming along the sides well after all of us had left the water. *"Cadet, jaldi bahar aao*[2], shouted the irate Instructor. It was then that N beckoned to the instructor.

What had happened was that the impactful and angular entry into the water after the jump had caused N's swimming trunks to split across the middle. Further, he had also ditched the trunks inside the pool and needed a towel to cover up for exiting the water.

N, for sure, left his jump mark in the pool that day!

□

1. A Hindi phrase meaning 'Keep standing straight'.
2. A Hindi phrase meaning 'Come out quickly'.

ERASE IT!

The 6th and last Term had started for us at our Tri-services Training Academy. The curriculum consisted mainly of individual Service subjects for us cadets (allotted for the three Defence Services of Army, Navy and the Air Force). Both classroom and practical training schedules were implemented by the respective Training Teams at the Academy. While this meant olive green combat fatigue rigs for the Army Cadets and overalls for the Air Force guys doing their glider training, Navy cadets could attend classroom instructions in the standard Academy Khaki Dress uniforms with the occasional PT rigs required for seamanship training at the nearby Sailing Bay area. Minor ribbing amongst us was common, regarding the relative toughness or comfort associated with the training environment for the three respective services.

However, the intensity of such contrasting environments was nowhere more brought home than by the specific directives given by the ACA[1] of the Academy after the first movie night in our 6th (senior most) Term.

All cadets had to view the movies screened regularly on Saturdays and Sundays at the huge Academy auditorium. The ACA was required to pass various directives for the coming Monday routine for all 6th Termers and sterner 'settling' of disciplinary issues for other junior cadets of the Academy, at the end of the movie.

For us 6th Termers, the instructions after the first movie

1. Academy Cadet Adjutant, who is an important 6th Term cadet appointment.

screening in the Term went like this: "Sixth Termers please listen—Army cadets are to carry their FSMOs[1] and rifle slings for Bayonet practice on Monday, Air Force cadets to report to Glider Dome sharp at 7 o'clock morning on Monday and Naval cadets to carry two HB pencils and an eraser for chart work."

To say that this brought the house down would be an understatement!

Later on, after the huge number of cribbing and ribbing by the Army and Airforce cadets, I tried to put it as wisely as I thought: "The pencil is mightier than the sword."

□

1. Field Service Marching Order is a specific kit and rig for Army cadets.

JUMP OFF!

We were in our Sixth and last Term at our Training Academy. Life was a breeze since we were the 'kings' of the Academy and only had less than six months to pass out after three long, eventful and arduous years of physical, mental and team toughening training. However, there was also the mandatory Test involving a feet-first smooth jump off the10m Diving Board into the Swimming Pool below.

Now, even some of the best swimmers baulked at this gravity-aided free fall into water from a three storeys building height. I had cleared the mandatory 50m Breast Stroke and 7m Jump Tests in my previous Terms with some difficulty and had some apprehensions about this Test from 3 metres higher up. The trick, as I repeatedly told myself, was to tag along after a confirmed 'jumper', and take the plunge without much thought or time for any nervousness.

So, there we were on an early morning Jump Test class at our Academy Swimming Pool. I was on the 10m board, shuffling ahead slowly behind two of my course-mates, cadets R and S. Now, I knew that S was a weak swimmer while R, who was the CSM[1] (Cadet Sergeant Major) of our Squadron[2], was pretty strong in the water. Since R was right in front of me, I was confident of my first attempt to jump immediately after R

---

1. The CSM is an important 6th Term cadet appointment of each Squadron. He is good in PT and games and is the enforcer of discipline and toughening up of junior cadets.
2. The Academy is divided into Battalions, which consist of 4 Squadrons each.

took the plunge. But I was in for a surprise!

S, who was one of the weakest swimmers and jumpers of the Squadron, fumbled around a bit at the concrete board edge. However, after considerable goading and cajoling from R, S sailed through the air to a splashdown some 30 plus feet below. R followed immediately after, with his characteristic smooth entry into the pool below.

I, who had my mind made up by this time, needed to take just three steps towards the board edge and the fourth in the air, for clearing my 10m Jump Test. As I neared the edge, I could make out the Swimming Instructor down below, gesticulating towards the water and then towards me. A little flummoxed, I peered down to see R thrashing around in the water just nearly below the 10M board edge. Adding to my astonishment and consternation was the fact that the Swimming Instructor jumped into the pool to retrieve the "strong" swimmer R and thereafter also S, and get them to the side of the pool. As the tension of these events started to begin clouding my confidence, I said a small mental prayer and could finally execute a near-perfect jump at the first blow of the Instructor's whistle.

As events transpired, what happened became clearer. S, after jumping into the water from the board, had delayed his leg kicks upwards whilst sinking towards the 16 odd feet deep swimming pool bottom. Thereupon, as R hit the water and he started sinking after impact, S was on his way up right below him. As R's legs hit S on the head, in panic, S grabbed hold of R's legs. The result was inevitable, and R had to ship some water along with S.

But then, what are Academy course mates for!

□

CROSSLINE!

The Sixth Term at our Tri-service training Academy was the last one over a three year eventful sojourn across the preparatory path for our future careers in the three disparate services of the Army, Navy and the Air Force. United and moulded through a common ethos, bound by loyalty as a course, we were, now inexorably approaching the penultimate end of an incomparable journey – one which was to be etched in our minds till the last breath.

We the Naval cadets, had a final event to showcase – the 'Crossing the Line' ceremony. This was an age-old tradition, wherein ships at sea, which were in the process of crossing the Equator, held a jamboree of mirth, play-acting and ribbing of mainly the Ship's officers. The whole procedure was overseen and directed by a crew member acting out the part of the Lord of the Seas—Neptune (or Lord Varuna in Hindu mythology). And, of course, the Lord had his consort Salacia (or Varuni in contemporary Hindu lore), along with his courtiers; the Queen had her maids, guards, etc. Finally, the event's end was heralded by the award of the precious certificates for crossing the Equator, to all and sundry on board the vessel.

The particular event was to be presented by us, the Naval cadets of the Course, just next to the Academy lake (which also served as our boatmanship and seamanship training venue).

I had been selected to play the role of the better half – Varuni[1]. Although my bit was restricted to sitting on a throne

1. The consort of Lord Varuna.

next to Lord Varuna[1] on the dias and looking 'queenly', it did require some detailed preparation—donning of make-up, including mascara, subtle lipstick shade and a wig. Even the dress to be worn had to be well-researched and as accurate as possible according to mythology and tradition. Since the Queen's and her two maids' roles were the only female ones enacted by an all-male cadets group, we had been sounded by our Instructors that these were specifically challenging acts to perform.

So there I was, sitting across from our Officer-in-Charge of training-Cdr M (an Education branch officer), discussing the nuances of the dress to be worn for my role in the landmark, or better still—the 'sea buoy' event.

"See S, we need to show the Queen as a being of the oceans and seas, and dress accordingly", said the Cdr. I racked my brains for a solution, all the while reminiscing about my maternal grandfather who we had been told had long ago played female roles in plays.

"Sir, I feel seaweeds and suchlike are apt probably for the dress material", said I, on the spur.

"Seaweeds – how on Earth do we get those here. We just have a lake, which should not be having seaweeds – only maybe some green algae or similar plant life", retorted M.

I ruminated some more, aware of the tension slowly spreading across the normally unflustered face of Cdr M. "C'mon S, you all will soon be fighting wars-this dress thing should not be an impasse", muttered M. True to our Academy's never-say-die attitude, I assured him that I would come up with something.

"You have three days S, our final Naval Training Team event is on Saturday. The Commandant will be the Chief Guest-it is a matter of our pride and honour, please remember", said Cdr M as I left his office.

---

1. The Hindu God of the seas.

I was already through with my thinking regarding the Queen's dress, by the time I returned to my Squadron cabin. Summoning three juniors, I instructed them to gather as many marigold flowers (It was winter, and the Squadron lawn areas were bright with the orange-yellow flowers) as possible and deposit them to me by evening. I also called my flank Second Termer and asked him to cut about ten odd two-feet lengths of doubled up threads, using his and my hausiffs. Nobody asked any reason – for them it was an order from 'God'.

And this 'God' would need the help of the real one, as events unfolded!

Over the next two days, I tried to put my plan into action. I had envisaged a hoola-hoop like a skirt (remembered from the Tahitian young ladies of the movie *The Caine Mutiny*) made from marigold flowers skewered, through with the thread lengths. All the ten 'flowery braids' would then be tied at the waist to a belt. This, to my mind, was the closest to 'seaweed and suchlike' –after all who would notice this inconsistency in the larger scheme of things.

But like the vagaries of a sudden storm at sea, things came to naught. The flowers wilted (we did not have any fridges in our cabins) despite the cool weather—the petals slowly disintegrating over the next two days. To add to my woes, some of the double threads broke due to the flowers' weight. So, when the flank Second Termer suggested at midnight previous to my deadline day that I should have gone in for artificial flowers and thin ropes instead of threads, it was rubbing salt over wounds.

On the third day morning I reported dejectedly to Cdr M that I had failed in my efforts. "C'mon S, life is sometimes like that. We fail only to rise. Do not worry – I will ensure we achieve the best", came the Commander's surprising reply.

Come afternoon, and as I walked slowly to his office again, I was still kicking myself for my non-working grandiose idea.

"Come S, your idea of a sea-associated dress is wonderful. Here, I got these from my daughter's friend." said the smiling Cdr M. And staring me in my face was a brightly coloured turquoise skirt patterned with weed-like strands shimmering against what looked a watery background!

The 'Crossing the Line' ceremony went off smoothly with no strong headwinds. We changed our clothes after the event, with me scrubbing cheeks off mascara, and headed for a sumptuous breakfast table.

We were feted by each one of our instructors, especially the ones who had acted out female roles.

Yes, sometimes 'skirting' the issue does help the line crossing!

□

NEVLA!

We were at the fag-end of the final Sixth Term at our Tri-Service training Academy. It was now all about preparations for the Term-end Camp. The Camp schedule started with visits to various Army and Air Force bases nearby the Academy. Included in the itinerary were Battle Tank firings and superb aerobatics show by the recently inducted supersonic fighters of the Air Force. We as Naval cadets took them all in, along with the sumptuous spreads at lunches hosted by the respective Services' Messes.

It was now the turn for the whole Course to visit ships and submarines at the Bombay Naval base. The Naval cadets were eager beavers about learning on actual ships and submarines, despite the relatively uncomfortable microclimate inside various Naval craft berthed at Dry Docks. The Army and Air Force guys, however, were not very pleased, given that they were used to vast open skies and land terrain and the cramped and occasionally greasy innards of ships and submarines were anything but that.

While we were billeted on-board a large Submarine Depot Ship for our sea sortie, the Army and Air Force Course-mates were divided amongst a frigate and destroyer for their maiden sea experience. A three-day exercise at sea followed, with us Naval cadets being given bunks and wash spaces located at the lowermost living quarters deck. For us, it was a fun trip, and the very basic facilities of bathing inside empty oil drums and closing up with the sea duty watches round-the-clock, was chalked up to experiential learning for our soon-to-be Naval futures. Seamanship drills, anchoring practices, star navigations, steering and conning orders, drills, etc., were observed with fascination and alacrity.

So, it was with slightly heavy hearts that the Naval cadets disembarked to land at the Bombay port, and gathered back for the rest of our training program, to be conducted on-board the harbour berthed ships over the next few days. The Army and Air Force cadets had meanwhile, returned to the Academy for their residual Camp training schedules. But we were told by some of our instructors that most of them had sullen looks after their recently completed first sortie at sea.

The Naval cadets were the last to return to the Academy after the Camp completion. Now, all Academy Squadrons had an in-house announcing system with Second Termers doing the shouted out announcements under the directives of the senior Termers. And so it transpired that all Squadrons could be heard announcing the return of the Naval Sixth Termers. We got back with our other two Services' Term mates and started exchanging notes.

Most non-Naval course mates then started their litany of complaints—rationed bathing and toilet flushing water at sea as well as the rolling and heaving causing poor appetites and some even poorer sleep. Quite a few came out saying that they were bitten by rats. As we tried to reason that rats were integral to ships from time immemorial (with most ships also having a countering pet cat on-board), we realised our entreaties were falling on deaf ears.

To balance their grievances, but ending up adding salt to their wounds, we informed that none of the Naval cadets had incurred the 'honour' of a rat-bitten toe or fingertips, even though we were sailing on a much older ship with less refined creature comforts.

It was then that the CSM (a dynamic Army cadet) of our

Course and a close friend of myself, came up with a unitary jewel: "C'mon guys, how can they be bitten? They are 'Nevlas' (Hindi for mongooses) who hunt and feast on rats. How dare those critters even touch their shadows!"

We 'Nevlas' took a bow for this simple but super effective act of Inter-services Jointmanship!

□

Section-2

UP SAIL!

We had just joined the Cadet Training Ship for our six-month-long on-board sojourn before stepping forth into a full-fledged life in the Navy. Life was a bit tough-with chock-full schedules of early morning Physical Training, seamanship evolutions, deck cleaning stints, classes on a plethora of diverse subjects; and of course, the all-important regular sailing sea sorties.

I had joined a bit late on-board, compared to my other batch mates. I got into the groove of things, under the tough and rough guidance of the Cadets' Petty Officer-in-Charge P. One fine day, we were occupied with deck cleaning and metal surface chipping, a little late into the afternoon. Our in-charge Petty Officer P was monitoring the activities with an eagle-eye out for any shirkers.

As he approached me (I was scraping up the loose chipped metal dust), he yelled: "Cadet G, get a shailll." Now, I knew that there was a locker aft on the Quarterdeck where the sail and riggings for some Enterprise sailboats were stowed. So I got up, and quickly made my way towards the stern of the ship. I could hear the Petty Officer repeating: "Get a shailll, Cadet G", behind me.

I took out the mainsail along with its attached mast and staggered up from the Quarterdeck to the HELO Deck. I had my task cut out in balancing the long sail-mast combine on my shoulders. But to my surprise, the Petty Officer was giving me a quizzical look and yelled even louder: "Cadet G, I told you to get a shaiill." "What the heck, that's what I am carrying over the past five minutes", I thought.

One of my batch mates was going by, with a heavy empty brass shell on his shoulder (a task awarded by Petty Officer P as a punishment for some snafu). As he passed, he whispered: "He means the shell", nodding towards Petty Officer P.

Click! The key turned in the lock. After stowing back the boat sail-mast in its rightful place, I made my way to an alley outside the Officers Wardroom, where the huge empty shells stood in a row, waiting for our shoulders.

It, later on, dawned on me that Petty Officer P's English dialect and accent were, to put it succinctly, a little drawn out. It was still maintained as such when many years later he hailed me when our paths crossed inside a Naval Dockyard.

The word 'shell shocked' became acutely entrenched in my mind from that day!

□

CAT'S PAW!

Our training on-board the Navy's Cadet Training Ship was coming to an end; rudimentary classroom and practical training on seamanship, navigation, boat-handling, bridgework, and watches in Machinery Room and on Main Switch Board had been about completed, bar the final assessment exams. A lot of days spent at sea had injected enough sea air and significant saltwater (specifically on rough sea sorties) into our energetic 21-22-year-old minds and bodies. The odd 'sessions[1] on jetties continued and we had all become accustomed to carrying super heavy ship's guns' shell cases and also adjusting to the various quirks of diverse officers and sailors staff of the ship.

One main event still had to be ticked off—the ubiquitous 'Cat's Paw'[2]. The evolution was initiated with a batch of five of us, under the able guidance of Sub Lt. M, aboard a Whaler (that tried and tested sea vessel from long ago). We were lowered early morning from our Mother Ship some miles off Goa to make our way back to the ship's berth at Marmagao Port. The distance had to be covered using oars, and as far as possible by sunset as the boat was bare bones without any Navigation lights or any power-driven propulsion. Rations provided were also very basic—fruits, biscuits, sandwiches and, of course, drinking water.

---

1. These are toughening up physical exercises including front rolling on a cemented jetty or carrying heavy brass shells on shoulders by the trainee cadets.
2. A 'cat's paw' refers to a light wind ruffling the sea surface in irregular patches during a calm.

Initially, the going was pleasant, with a slightly cool breeze making the humid weather bearable. We kept straining at our oars enthusiastically, while our affable Sub Lt. kept chatting away; now he was less of the Master-of-Ceremonies of jetty sessions galore. However, as the Sun rose towards its zenith, its hot rays started scorching the back of our necks, and with the wind also dying down, we started realising that the cat had started sheathing her claws back inside her paws.

The sea became choppier and white horses[1] were all around. The Goa seas (which seems magically beckoning from the *feni*-soaked views of umpteen beachside tourists at Miramar or Bogmalo) have a wicked swell, which kept rolling our boat slowly but surely. Seafarers as we had to be, and a major part of our sea rowing still left, we tried to renew our efforts at our oars. Our Sub Lt. now took over the rudder tiller control, and started shouting out encouragement and the near metronomic 'in…out' for the correct timing of our oar strokes.

It was now lunchtime by landlubbers' routine, but the sea Gods seemed to have other plans for us. Most of us were already slightly green in the rolling and pitching Whaler. One Cadet B was specifically sick and could not hold back much food or water inside him. Even our Sub Lt. kept retching off and on. Two of us, including Cadet K and myself were in the best fettle and managed to keep our innards from throwing up.

Sub Lt. M (a very fit athlete and avid yachtsman) could not hold back any longer and after stripping off his T-shirt, dived into the sea for a refresher bath. After about five minutes he exhorted us to take turns for the sea bath. And lo and behold! Cadet K's lean muscular body arrowed inside the water, and I followed suit. The Sub Lt. clambered back aboard and with renewed vigour coordinated the by-now slower oar pulling, and controlling the boat's heading towards Marmagao. The shoreline was visible and bar the acutely seasick Cadet B, the others dug in to keep time with the Coxswain of the boat, Sub Lt M.

1. These are waves with white surf at the tops.

Now, K and myself were keeping pace in the water, swimming alongside the Whaler, oblivious of everything but the welcome coolness of the sea and enjoying the roll-less look at the azure sky. I, a bit more laid back, slowed down at an easier pace, and tried out back floating on the dense salty waves—it was now near magical.

But as the boat pulled away, with K nearly glued to its side in the water, I suddenly realised I had fallen back considerably, and the others in the Whaler seemingly indifferent to my status, or so I felt. About three boat lengths away now, I started panicking. I started increasing my stroke rate, keeping my eternal optimist's flag up, expecting to catch up soon. However, this did not happen, with the rest of the boat crew seemingly re-energised and pulling away faster!

No choice, I stopped my swimming strokes, and like a 'dead sinker', started waving and hollering out loudly. About 15 seconds passed, and now I was desperate, even thinking of the sharks prevalent in these waters. I could make out that Cadet K was also back on the boat.

Then-whoosh, the boat's Lifebuoy came whizzing through the air towards me, with its tethering line attached and uncoiling as it floated towards me. I snatched it and clung on like a goose barnacle.

As I was pulled back on board– I realised with a subtle irony that:

The Sea did not make me sick
Allowed me the swimming stroke kick
But I was to be the pick
For a seemingly wrong end of the stick
Happily got life buoyed in time's nick.

It also made me realise the truth of the time-tested adage of 'being in the same boat'!

□

HIGH STAKES!

We were Cadets on-board the recently commissioned Training Ship of the Navy. The Ship was based at Cochin (now Kochi). The Naval harbour afforded a picturesque view of the incoming Entrance Channel as well as the in-cutting of the Arabian Sea further inland to form the famous backwaters—a tourist's must-see. However, for us this pleasure was mostly short lived as we ground our days and nights through early morn PT, chipping away at rusted surfaces on-board, back-to-back classroom periods and the ubiquitous jetty sessions. These sessions entailed rolling up and down on the Ship's adjoining jetty and further stiffer tasks of carrying weighty shells on our youthful shoulders. They were mostly administered and supervised by Sub Lts. borne on our Ship for obtaining their Watch keeping tickets.

Now, we also followed a Three Watch roster[1] to carry out duties in the harbour as part of the Ship's Duty Watch. These included manning the Gangway, assisting the Logistics Officer in accounting for various rations and other supplies as and when they came on board, and also the mandatory Fire Exercise daily.

One fine day, I and another batch mate B were on the Duty Watch. We had mostly spent an uneventful day at the Gangway, and as evening approached, we were trying to enjoy the fine sea breeze wafting across the Quarter Deck, where we were positioned. However soon, our reverie (sort of) was

1. Each cadet had to be on duty once in 3 days

interrupted when we were summoned by the OOD post-haste to the gangway. We rushed along and were instructed to man the Duty Whaler boat, which was tied up alongside the Ship's seaward side. Even as we lowered ourselves to the Whaler via the hanging Jacob Ladder, the OOD directed us towards the Fishing Stakes, of which there were numerous, right near the Thevara Bridge about half a mile from our Ship.

The four-man crew including us two and the maintenance staff of the boat (again rooky sailors also undergoing training on-board) quickly untethered the boat and using the outboard motor sped towards the Stakes. We were also in constant communication with the Ship's OOD who by and by informed us that Sub Lt. M (recently joined the Ship) had been windsurfing in the Channel and had not returned to the Ship till then.

It was slowly growing darker and my batch mate took over the OBM-cum-Rudder control from me (he was more adept at boatmanship) and lined us up towards the Fishing Stakes, which were now just about a cable away.

Lo and behold! We saw a strange sight—the Surfboard along with the sail was partially submerged in the water and Sub Lt. M was sitting like a roosting seagull on one of the Fishing Stakes! The water was swirling pretty fast around the Stakes and we had our work cut out.

My batch mate, again the more efficient 'boater' quickly rounded around the Stakes, and under M's guidance, we threw a Life Buoy towards him. He caught it neatly and had to nearly fly off the Stake (the smooth and somewhat jagged surface of the vertical Stake did not afford much grip and could cause injury as well). In the end, we retrieved him, and also could complete the tougher task of securing and hauling the much heavier Surfboard along with its Sail onto our Whaler. The rest was routine returning to the Ship where the OOD gave M a small 'bottle' and that was that.

But a happier turn of events happened after this incident, wherein M was softer on the two of us during the umpteen jetty sessions thereafter.

We had had a first-time Naval experience where the 'stakes' had been definitely high!

□

SEA DRUNK!

Our batch of eighty-odd cadets was borne on the Navy's recently acquired Training Ship. The curriculum included extensive hands-on Seamanship and Navigation experience, apart from regular classroom instructions. And, not to forget, getting our sea-legs, and transitioning from landlubbers to seafarers.

Life was both tough and enlightening – from Semaphore and Morse Code reading to Bridge work to doing watches in the Engine Room and the Main Switchboard. We were considered junior to mostly everyone on-board and could be ordered around by all and sundry.

Our Petty Officer In-charge, however, was a very empathetic but firm administrator, and ensured we did not get pushed around too much. Regular Enterprise sailing and Whaler rowing added to our outdoor waterborne activities and we also enjoyed our trip to two ports abroad towards the end of our training sojourn.

Somewhere in the middle of our training term, our Ship was operating off the Western coast, and after completion of a two-week-long sea sortie chock-full of activities for us, we were looking forward to our three-day stopover at Goa. Now, Goa, also known as Hawaii of the East, was an ideal port for rest and recreation on a static platform after the rougher seas we had recently encountered. Divided into three Duty Watches, each one of us were assured of two-days off to enjoy our hard-earned Liberty period on the beaches of Goa.

Some of our course mates had done their previous initial training at the Naval Academy at Goa. Most of them fairly knew nearly all of the beaches of both North and South Goa. Their knowledge of the locations for cheaper beach shacks serving food and drinks was to come very handy for our significantly limited budgets of fixed monthly pocket monies.

Since I was a newcomer to the place, I had decided that it would make sense to tag along with a bunch of cadets, some of whom were alumni of the Goa Academy.

So, it transpired that we travelled across both North and South Goa beaches, soaking in the sun, sea, and sand. And, boy, we gorged on the seafood—prawns, lobsters, barracuda and other bounty of the sea. On my second day out, I was strolling along with another of my close friends at one of South Goa's most scenic and crowded beaches. Both were first-timers at this haven for tired souls, and on mutual agreement, we decided we must try out the famed Feni[1].

We bought two small intricately and beautifully designed bottles (alcohol is pretty cheap in Goa). To add the touch of 'Hawaii', we stripped to our swimming trunks and started wading out in the water, all the while quaffing copious amounts of the pungent liquid.

The Sun was still not fully down and we could feel some heat on our necks. By then, the fermented cashew liquor started taking hold, and as we dipped our heads into the salty seawater, the effect was indescribable. We were in a mix of light-headedness, floating as if on air and feeling groggy as well. Cadet C, my friend, exclaimed that why go back to anywhere else, and insisted we stay and spend the night looking at the stars while lying on the heavenly sands of Bogmalo beach. Now, I was only slightly less sloshed, but had the innate survival instinct to realise that we needed to be back on board before the hours of liberty ended.

---

1. A traditional Goan alcoholic drink made from cashew or toddy palm brew.

I, thus, did have to make some efforts to gather ourselves back and return to our parent ship in time to beat the bell. One of our Course mates, we learned later, had returned much after the deadline, and flushed after a peg too much of Vodka. This caused us all to have an early morning rolling session on the jetty adjoining the Ship before we departed from the port.

In retrospect, we could, however, never quite analyse as to which drink caused the heavenly effects that evening in Goa—the Sea or Feni, or both!

And it made me realise that sometimes the drink could be as 'fathomless' as the deep Sea!

□

THE NAVY STATE INSECT!

Five of us were Midshipmen on-board a large frigate, which had recently been inducted into the Navy at Bombay. The ship had had more than a fair share of sailings, both independently and with the Fleet. It was good for us in order to develop our sea legs, although it curtailed our exuberance of 21-year-olds exploring the dream city of Bombay (the name-change was to come much later). The veteran and soft-spoken Captain treated us like his children and had given us a free hand in having fun, along with gaining knowledge during our six-month-long on-board tenure.

The Executive Officer was a large, bearded and swarthy aviator, with a booming voice to match. He had a colourful past and was a thorough professional. He generally left us to be trained under the tutelage of the ship's Navigator. However, he was very particular about us attending the periodic Request men and Defaulters schedule. This exercise was to be of great help in our naval life later on.

I was the lone Midshipman-of-the-Watch in the Bridge, during every event of preparing the ship for entering or leaving the harbour. I used to assist the Sub Lieutenant-of-the-Watch during the entire duration of each of these evolutions. Just before the ship cast-off from alongside, the three Heads—the Executive Officer, the Engineering Officer and the Electrical Officer—made their respective departmental readiness reports to the Captain on the Bridge.

During one such instance, the Executive Officer lingered

on in the Bridge during the casting-off sequence of the frigate. I was immediately wary, in anticipation of any questions from him, since as a Mid, one was expected to know everything under the sun. Time went by as the Bridge staff got along with the conning and engine orders directed by the Captain for getting underway and out through the harbour channel. Just when I was lapsing into a more relaxed frame of mind, the dreaded beckoning came from the Executive Officer.

I sidled near him to a corner windscreen of the Bridge He looked a bit thoughtful and pointed to the corner windscreens. "Smudged glass—not clean enough, or is he trying to quiz me on some navigation mark[1] visible through the screen?" These were the thoughts in my mind as I racked my brains as to his yet unvoiced query.

"See that?" Softly spoke the ship's Commander, directing my gaze to something on the glass pane. I craned my neck and tried looking closer. The best I could make out was a speck on the glass screen. Silence followed, but I was not the wiser. Suddenly, the Executive Officer said: "Does the mosquito not make the Mercedes Benz insignia?"

Whoom—it hit me! It was only later on that I could realise the Commander's intelligent interpretation—the splayed hind feet of the mosquito neatly making the famous 3-star Merc logo. More so—the Benz insignia depicts the three media of Air, Land and Sea, which is where the Navy operates!

Thereafter, the much-maligned mosquito had a new fan following!

□

1. These include various kinds of buoys, lighthouses, etc.

PILGRIM'S PROGRESS!

The five of us were Midshipmen on-board the latest commissioned frigate of the Navy. Fresh after an exacting training schedule on-board the Cadet Training Ship over the past six months, we found our newfound Mids' pips and access to the Officers Ward Room on board, quite a liberating experience. The ship's Captain—a very polished and seasoned professional—was childless and we five were as good as his 'kids'. In fact, on our first meeting with him, he advised us to learn well but above all—to ENJOY better. We followed these instructions to nearly a T—especially the 'enjoyment' part.

Being a new ship, we sailed regularly; our youthful lungs and veins thus continued their saltwater and sea breeze aeration. Watches on the Bridge, Ops Room, and at times in the WT Office and EW Room (here we chatted with the SCO2, who was our mentor and friend all in one), enabled brushing up of our cadets' days' skills on-board a leading Capital Ship at sea and in harbour. Some of us also became more observant of the mannerisms, quirks and small foibles of the various OOWs, whom we assisted during respective Watches.

Now, once, we had been on a longish month-long-cross coast sea sortie, away from our base port. After an intensive exercise schedule with the fleets of either coast Commands, we entered Madras (now renamed Chennai) port for a much-awaited stopover. Three full days of alongside break and shore liberty beckoned the officers and sailor crew of the ship.

Normally, the five of us shared a 3 Watch Roster in harbour

for MOD duties, with me the loner in one. However, since this was our first visit to Madras, all five of us were excused of the harbour duties for the first day at this southern port.

Agog with the exuberance and curiosity of 20-21-year-olds, we were on a high, with cash in pocket (the Rs.1500 as monthly stipend went a long way in the late 80s). We had a quick tete-a-tete in our 'private JOM" to chalk out our POA[1] before hitting the city's popular Marina Beach.

When, without warning, an intercom phone call from the EXO informed that the Captain had arranged a full luxury bus for all officers to visit Tirupati—the famous and very popular Dham[2], which was a must-do on any pilgrim's schedule. This was nothing less than a bombshell for us Snotties, rivaled in intensity only by probably the ship's main gun firing at sea.

Finally, with a vote through hands-show, the decision to miss the bus trip was taken. The senior-most in our group conveyed this contentious news to the EXO and escaped with a minor 'bottle' (the No. 2 on-board finally counted on the Captain's fondness for us, to excuse our non-inclusion in the pilgrim group).

As it transpired, we could have a fairly good time at Burma Bazaar (a haven for 'grey market' goods in pre-liberalisation India when foreign stuff was a rarity for potential customers), lolled and relaxed on the clean sands of the city's beach, and quaffed a few beers in a local pub (our pockets did not permit the pricey up-market bars). Some of us also risked the ire of the haggling Burma Bazaar vendors to purchase white Naval uniform cloth at pretty low prices (mainly ordered by some of the Ship's officers too). As the sky turned redder for evening and sunset, and a cool but balmy sea breeze blew, we congratulated ourselves over our decision to stick to our plan for our much due liberty.

---

1. Plan of action.
2. There are four major Dhams amongst Hindus. Each such Dham is a revered pilgrimage site.

As we made our way back to our Ship, we were deliberating over what liquor to imbibe to go with the night's dinner Menu in the Wardroom. Maybe a nice movie on the VCR too– surmised Mid A (those were the late 80s and CDs or Netflix had not yet hit India).

Even As A pushed open the Wardroom entry door, we could feel a hushed silence inside, with none of the usual talks and chatter audible. The full Officers' strength was seated around on the sofas, with mainly looks of disconcert.

As requested the Wardroom Steward to ask for drinks all around, we were narrated the frightening and sobering turn of events which had transpired over the day and evening, for the bus' travellers.

Somewhat short of their destination, the bus had met with a pretty serious accident. Some of them had sustained minor injuries but the driver was badly injured. A concerted decision to return without the Dham visit was taken, once the wounded were tended to at a wayside clinic. The travellers had reached the ship just about half an hour before we did.

Anyway, beers were opened, whiskeys sipped (even the hard-core teetotallers had a peg that night) and the ubiquitous Pork Luncheon Meat Eats wolfed down by eager and hungry 'pilgrims' and beachcombers alike.

Overnight, I thought out loud:

"Did the missing Snotties anger the Gods or were we the chosen few to escape that fateful and ominous visit to the Dham while in Madras..?"

□

CAT WALKING!

We were five of us, as Midshipmen onboard a barely two-year-old frigate of the Navy. Life was a step up from the Naval cadets' time on Training Ships. However, we were still the junior-most on the officers' list. Considered to be youngster Snotties—immature, but required to know everything under the Sun, so to say. We had a strict Training Officer (the ship's Navigator), and also an empathetic and jovial mentor in the EWO.

Recently commissioned, the ship was fully operational and we were mostly at sea, in more ways than one. Divided into three groups, we rotated our sea duty watches between the Forecastle as assistant to the Gunnery Officer, on Bridge to assist the OOW, sometimes in the WTO, and at times on the Quarter Deck with the ASWO. Learning the ropes was our credo, with occasions for merriment in the Ward Room and the JOM, where we were billeted.

Now, we were allotted the JOM on one of the ship's wings, just one deck below the Bridge. And, the Captain's Sea Cabin was right opposite ours, on the opposite wing. The JOM had lots of spare bunks, despite our considerable crowd of five. There were also enough lockers for storing personal belongings, not that we had much, being the start of our earning Naval careers.

The JOM had three-tiered bunk levels, and Mid V occupied one directly underneath me (I had the middle one). Owing to the four-hour-long tricks of a three watches system at sea, one or two bunks out of our five were always empty.

However, Mid V had the watch next to next the one I had. So it was that when I returned from my watch at nights, Mid V used to be fast asleep.

We were once on a weeklong sea-sortie, and the schedule was chock full of exercises with the full Fleet. The Fleet Commander had also visited our ship on one occasion by helo, and all of us tried to catch up as much sleep as possible (which at times amounted to a daily 6-7 hours). I had the graveyard shift one night, and after finishing, I came back to the JOM. Without switching on any lights (we had an in-house dictum not to disturb other sleeping Snotties), I arrived at the foot of my bunk group.

By habit, I glanced at the bottom bed, and lo and behold! Mid V was missing!!

Thinking that he probably had gone to the heads, I clambered up to my bunk and snuggled inside my blanket (being a new ship, and the punkah louvers directly above me on the deckhead, it used to get quite chilly at night). Ten minutes passed, and I was on the verge of dropping off to sleep when I realised that V had still not returned.

Now, V was a pretty active and fit guy, and unless he had the loosies, I surmised that he should not have been gone away to the heads for so long. Stranger things could happen, so I kept awake for another fifteen minutes, to be satisfied with V's return.

However, the bottom bunk remained empty.

Buying the logic of two heads better than one, and that return from a heads visit was overdue, I climbed down and shook awake my next bunkmate—Mid K. He grumbled—he also had the next-to-next 8 am watch and needed his sleep. But as I conveyed the urgency, he was wide awake. After all, crew falling off ships at sea was not such a rare occasion, and this gave wings to our next actions. We decided we would scour the Bridge and Ops Room first (in case he had been given a 'punishment' watch by the Training Officer, a little 'wild' as Mid V was at times). Thereafter, we shared our searches in the Wardroom (in case he was catching up on a late late night movie) and the EW Office (our EWO was close to V, and often chatted up with him). But our efforts came to nought. And now we were really worried.

Before deciding to report to Bridge about missing V, Mid K suggested we cover the port and starboard forward catwalks as well—just in case. As I hurried towards the port one, and about to open the bulkhead Door leading from the superstructure to the catwalk, the door smoothly swung inwards.

And, like a spirit of the night, I was confronted by the sight of Mid V stepping inside the inner alleyway from the port Catwalk! And his eyes were closed and he was ASLEEP!

We later learned about his very infrequent sleepwalking incidents. God, he was lucky that night that he had not fallen overboard—the guardian stars over the sea sky were surely watching over him that night.

We, of course, had a celebration of sorts with canned beer in our JOM, when we returned to harbour. And, I exchanged bunks with V, to reduce chances of any such further nightly sojourns.

It also brought about the new adage in my mind—'Pussyfooting on the Catwalk'!

□

SNAKE ALIVE!

I had been deputed to a coastal Naval detachment in South India. The place itself was hard to reach by train-it required a change-over to metre gauge track, after travelling overnight from Madras, as it was called then. The adjoining small town was a semi rural location, with the charm of green farm lands and tiny shops in the adjoining hinterland.

We officers were messed in an old state government guesthouse bungalow, while the sailor staff was billeted in various buildings within the Detachment complex. Security was afforded by solid concrete walls, and wire fencing at some points. Armed sentries patrolled the entry/exit gates, and a machine gun post had also been installed on the rooftop of one of the taller buildings.

All in all, a well organized set up had been created, somewhat like the Army camps across the country. Rations were transported by truck from Madras , once a month; while fresh rations , official and private mail (those were non internet and mobile phone days, so a lot of eagerly awaited personal correspondence had to be sent to and fro) and newspapers were delivered by the supply contractor once a week.

I was entrusted with the logistics management and Regulating Officer duties. This generally took up most of my working hours; off times were spent playing volleyball and football in the evenings and viewing the weekly movies on a locally rented VCR. Rum (the traditional Naval drink from times immemorial) ration quotas were distributed on a daily basis in the evenings.

Now, all Detachment personnel had to muster daily in the mornings at the big open grounds within the complex. This was vital–to do a head count, disseminate important messages and orders as well as to delegate the jobs for the day. Department wise sailors were grouped into platoons—the supervising Senior Sailor reported the parade state to me, and I in turn reported to the 2i/c of the Detachment.

One such fine morning on a slightly cloudy day (this part of the country had more than its share of annual rain), the sailors had more or less mustered, and the senior Petty Officers and Chief Petty Officers were just about readying for reporting to me. I was generally having a discussion with the Master Chief-at-Arms regarding tightening up of security (a few wild pigs had been espied trying to sneak into the precincts the night before). Suddenly I observed some hustling around in two of the mustered platoons-and soon a big inter platoon gap was created.

Then–lo and behold, a 3 metres long black snake slithered its way upfront along this gap in the 'parade ground'!! And the cobra's "mark of Vishnu" hood was just flaring up in the classic raised position.

Master Chief-at-Arms, ever alert and impassive, barked out orders to the LPM[1], who sprightly used a nearby stick to pin the business end of the serpent. The expert snake handler sailor (trained by default in the verdant and sometimes deadly long grasses of rural Kerala), gripped the tail end, and finally pushed the wriggling *Naja naja*[2] inside a hastily brought wooden box. Job done, the snake was carted outside and released away from the area in a grassy glade. Simon and Suxie would have been proud.

1. Leading Provost Marshal—a junior sailor who is the prime assistant and subordinate to the Master Chief-at-Arms.
2. Scientific name of the Indian Cobra.

This was the only time in my Naval tenure that I had witnessed the protector and abode of Lord Vishnu, trying to attend Both Watches[1]!

□

1. The muster of all personnel of afloat and ashore naval units as part of daily routine.

Section-3

SHOCKED!

We were—the around forty of us—in the starting end of our year-plus-long Technical Courses, after finishing our Midshipmen time on various ships. It was a happy gathering, as we were meeting after around a year from our Navy-initiating Sea Cadet days aboard our Training Ship. For the shaky legs and seasick prone of us, it was particularly gratifying to be back on terra firma, although it was foregone that many more sea-bound days would follow.

Our intensive course for learning the rudiments and marine applications of Electrical and Engineering theory had commenced. Routine-bound for various diverse classes, sports, Guard Room[1] duties and social callings and receptions, we were slowly but surely being further groomed into leaders for driving the future Navy.

It was around the middle of our course that the festival of Holi was around the corner. Most of us hailed from the Northern parts of India, where Holi was one of the two most important and much-celebrated festivals. The occasion usually brought with it gaiety, huge bonhomie, lots of colours smearing, mischief and good cheer with '*bhang*[2]' being drunk by many.

Our Officer-in-Charge at the Training School was a seasoned submariner, very erudite and royalty personified.

1. Every shore unit has an entrance gate with security guards. They operate from a small building called the Guard Room.
2. A traditional intoxicating drink brewed from cannabis.

The festival celebration preparations were, accordingly, laid out on a grand scale. Huge *shamianas*[1] had been erected, very high output stereo system rigged up, and umpteen drinks counters laid out. It was a day affair, and a lavish lunch was to follow the (un) choreographed celebratory rituals.

Around noon, we had already started off our rounds of greeting and exchanging colours with the other officers and their families, with great gusto. After about two hours of doing these rounds, we gathered back at the large playing grounds of the Base, for the drinks, music, and lunch, mostly in that order.

The boom box started playing out the choicest Bollywood Hindi songs, and the crowd started milling around. Most of us were, of course, downing our drinks, easing the intensity of the day as it grew warmer. Slowly and surely, people joined the dance floor, which was made of wooden platforms.

Less of dance and more PT combined with many flailing limbs, our youthful energy levels were unstoppable. In the middle of all this, some of us had espied an oval-shaped water pool nearby. Holi was not the same without dunking, and the more reticent of us got thoroughly wet in the mostly muddy pool water. Others were diversely drunk on copious amounts of beer or chandy (a typical beverage made by mixing beer with some aerated soda), and the pool water drinking was just some more grist for the mill.

Now, the area around the dance floor was adjoining the bar counters, connected through various un-metalled narrow strips of treaded dusty paths, We shared between us the dancing and fetching of beer bottles for the still-to-be sloshed amongst us, and the path strips were being frequently used. But the icing on our merrymaking cake was still to be had!

Lo and behold! Many of us started their dance steps in the middle of the connecting paths, much before reaching the

---

1. Indian ceremonial tent or awning.

dance floor, some even balancing as many as four beer bottles! Some of us (the less inebriated, that is) observed this but put it down to a drink too much along with the headiness of the occasion.

However, it was just before we were about to make our way towards the buffet lunch table that I stumbled upon the real reason. What had been happening was that a nearly naked electric wire (connecting up the Boom Box with the hastily set up electric switchboard) was snaking its way along one of the regularly trodden strips turning most of us, even ones with two left feet, into wannabe Michael Jacksons!

We had finally experienced what 220V 60Hz electric supply felt like!

□

UNSYNCHRONISED!

We had cleared our Mid Boards[1] and were now looking forward to a year-plus training course at various schools of the Navy. Somewhere around three months into our schedule, we were based at the Electrical and Electronics Training School. Here, the curriculum consisted of early morning PT (something the late 'birds' were loath to attend) or drill practice for Divisions, followed by intense classroom sessions till lunch. Evenings were mostly games, and weekends had occasional receptions and parties to attend.

Life was well organised, and many a holiday was spent visiting nearby tourist places. Some days, of course, one had to do duty at the Guard Room of the huge Base. There were also the few altercations with seniors, but which were reconciled over a beer glass at the Ward Room bar. Many of our seniors or SOGs as they were designated also shared interesting anecdotes with us over drinks, some of whom pretty salty too.

All in all, the times were good, and more so due to the huge-sized chicken *tandoori*[2] legs available at the base Club. These legs were so large, some of us contemplated that they belonged to the bevy of pink-billed flamingoes, which flocked regularly at the nearby salt-laden marshes visible from the Club premises!

One of our course mates, Sub Lt. DK was a BA graduate

1. All Midshipmen need to qualify an assessment by a Board, at the end of their five-month-long training period.
2. A very popular Indian dish wherein the chicken pieces are roasted in a clay oven after marination.

from the Tri-Service Academy, from where we had completed our initial military training about a year ago. He was trying to cope with the myriad subjects being taught as part of our course. These included diverse fields from sonar and sound theory to how generators and motors worked. Most instructors started with the basics, to get all BAs and BScs on the same level, before moving ahead to more complex developments.

Now, one of our instructors Lt. K was teaching us about Fleming's Left and Right-Hand Rules[1] (which seem easy but could affect some confusion after years when memory fades). He had, albeit, with much effort, got the class on an even keel about understanding the Rules, and had thereon moved on to teaching us the rudiments and theory of motor coils and synchros.

It was one of those Mondays where, after a weekend of hard partying and a gruelling early morning Divisions practice on the Drill Grounds, we had started to settle down into our first class of synchros and coils. It was a pretty large gathering of about 40 odd trainees in various states of enthusiasm and tiredness, with a few still scratching from the mosquito bites suffered at the Drill practice; some were even still in a semi-somnambulistic state. However, DK was right amongst the front-benchers, keen to imbibe the tough topics to be covered that class.

The not-so-happy looking instructor started his class and announced that we had better pay close attention since this was a challenging topic, and would find pride of place in the Question Paper for our assessment Tests scheduled very soon. We were soon in various degrees of using our cortical cells for listening, writing notes and sometimes surreptitiously whispering to our bench mates regarding the difficulties in absorbing the nuances of the topic. One course-mate, a

1. Two basic important principles underlying theory of electromagnetism.

habitual late riser, had to spring a leak, but even he was forced by the strict instructor to sit out the class before rushing to the loo.

And then it happened as the class came to a close, with many anxiously looking at our watches for the happy event of the bell ring. DK suddenly shot up ramrod-straight (he was a superb athlete), and stridently asked if he could ask an urgent query. The instructor gave an irritated look (he was anyway a grumpy sort) at him and nodded.

Bang came DK's query: "Sir, what is the topic you are teaching?"

For once, we were glad that the Instructor was ELECTRIFIED, and that is an understatement!

□

PLAY ON!

Our batch of Sub Lts. had just started our Technical Courses across various training schools of the Navy, spread over various locations in India. The first stop was at the Navy's Logistics and Supply branch's Base near Bombay, next to the sheltered rocky beaches adjoining the Arabian Sea.

It was the late 80's—computers and mobile phones had to still make their appearance in India. We, who were undergoing an Officer's capsule course in Naval Logistics, also had a course of fresh entry Naval Cooks and Stewards undergoing their concurrent training at the Base. These amateur cooks and stewards prepared and served exotic dishes for us to taste and assess—basically we were both gourmands and guinea pigs rolled into our early 20's youthful selves.

Life for us was fairly a cinch, with classroom instructions, some drill parades and regular weekend bashes at the Officers Wardroom Mess lawns. We had also heard of a Bollywood song starring a topmost actress, being picturised some years back at the beaches, which formed part of the private estate of the Base, and had lingering hopes of seeing similar events during our stint. Some had recently purchased mobikes, and these were admired by each of us, with some getting pillion rides on sojourns to the town outside the Base.

There were lots of playgrounds and courts for various racquet games at the Base. In fact, our Course Chief Instructor Officer insisted us to use these to keep our fitness levels in tip top shape. Most of us were very fit, and a few, who had a few

extra kilos piled on, did try their hands at Tennis, Badminton and Squash.

Now, the Squash courts were much in demand by many of us (except people like me), and one had to reserve these much in advance , especially on weekend afternoons when we were free of classroom assessment Tests (these generally happened on Saturday mornings). But the majority of us were more prone towards beach running and swimming (especially those who were planning to become Naval Divers in the future), or a game of relatively less technicality, football.

One fine day, two of us were sipping our orange squash drinks around 4 pm at the Officers Institute lawns, which was situated next to our residential building blocks. I was also observing, and pretty intrigued by the hordes of water birds, which roosted on the many trees lining the pathway near the Institute and near our accommodation apartments, the birds' guano droppings had nearly made half the roads' widths a gleaming white, which earmarked their patch of territory.

As I slowly sipped the last dregs of the very popular and refreshing squash drink, my colleague Sub Lt. RP suggested we try out a game of Squash (he was one of our best players). I had recently purchased a racquet, and needed to try it out. Never one to shy out of anything new, I immediately joined RP in ambling across to the nearby courts.

Although it was a Saturday, being a bit early in the evening, the courts were empty and after some practice shots, we started playing in earnest. Although I was fairly fit in spite of not being remarkable at a particular sport, I found myself a bit fatigued, but put it down to my novice efforts at playing this highly physical and technically demanding racquet game.

But after two games (I was, of course, beaten soundly by RP although he was probably playing his B game), I gave up. Apart from sweating profusely on this balmy and warm evening, I was also feeling somewhat queasy. Anyway, I gave myself credit for finally breaking the rubicon in this racquet sport that day.

It was only later on I realised the humour in the incident.

I had actually been Squashed either way, with Squash after Squash, on that Saturday evening 3 decades back!

□

BIRTHDAY BLUES!

The Technical Courses in the Navy for our batch of Sub Lts. had commenced; the starting end of the year-plus-long Course involved a stint at the Marine Engineering Training Base. We were all from the Executive branch of the Navy, and being aware of the rudiments of ship propulsion systems, auxiliary systems, damage control systems, organisation, etc., were all par for the course. The Course was designed to refresh and develop our about seven-month-old moulding and initiation during our training on-board the Navy's Cadet Training Ship.

Our routine was mostly like any Military Training Base—a judicious mixture of classroom and practical training, along with social events, sports, etc. We were housed in various apartments within the Base and dined at the Wardroom Mess. Some had already purchased motorbikes and were generous enough to share pillion rides for trips outside the Base to the nearby scenic town and adjoining areas of tourist interest. All in all—a very satisfactory schedule with the only anxious moments being the preparations for the Assessment Tests at the end of classroom instructions for each subject.

Now, the vast Base also had a club (we affectionately called it a *dhaba*) this enabled members to partake drinks, snacks and dinner as well as play the occasional Tambola[1] game. Most Northerners of our course satiated their *chicken-*

1. An Indian version of Bingo.

tikka[1] and *naan*[2] tastebuds at this place. The Southerners had to be satisfied with some *dosa*[3] and *vada*[4] items. But for all of us it was a haven—slightly away from some Instructors' eagle eyes, and also to let our hair down. The Club was overseen and supervised by one of our strictest Instructors, Cdr P.

It was March, and we were nearly at the long end of our Training Course. We had gathered at the club one evening essentially to celebrate my birthday. Lots of drinks were downed, and we had probably finished off the club's chicken menu stock. Further nightcaps followed, along with boisterous back slapping.

The Manager had to inform us that it was beyond the closing time when we made (some were staggering) our ways back to our cabins.

The next day was a working day, and in the forenoon was Instructor P's class on Damage Control. The subject was a tough one, and under P's relentless spectacled glare, it was all the more torturous. Anyway, we plodded through, with some still under a somnambulistic haze. It was nearing the class completion when the reverie of most of us was broken by the louder squeaky nasal high-pitched voice of P addressing the whole class. "What were you all doing at the club yesterday night? A case of late securing of bar and club premises has been reported to me", goaded P.

Slightly nonplussed by this sudden change in tack, most of us sat up from our slouched stances, waiting for further drama to unfold. It had after all been a full course affair at the club, and nobody wanted to fib on anyone. As seconds ticked away (I for one was awaiting the final bell, feeling slightly guilty), our class senior stood up and tried to explain that it was a get-together, one odd glass had broken by accident and

1. An Indian dish made of boneless chicken cooked in spicy marinade.
2. Oven-baked flatbread popular in Asia.
3. A South Indian dish like rice pancake.
4. A savoury fried snack from South India.

we regretted staying beyond closing hours. As P considered the reasonableness of this excuse like a judge for capital sentences, our course-mate Sub Lt M piped up: "We were singing happy birthday for one of us."

The ice was thus broken and P murmured: 'That's ok then...do not repeat late staying at the Club and break rules", as he walked out the classroom door.

The birthday song did save us the Blues, as did M!

□

BLOODY ENDING!

The Technical Courses for our batch of youthful and energetic Sub Lts. were in full swing. We were now into our final overs viz., training schedule at the various Schools, at a scenic South Indian port city. Navigation, Communication, ASW, Gunnery, Seamanship were now being absorbed with gusto, and sometimes ennui. Weekend assessment exams needed slogging, but all in all the stint was engaging and we had our moments of slack too.

Sub Lt. MS and I had formed a close duo, out to visit various tourist spots in and around the city. We had a handsome salary and dollops of energy, so our enthusiasm was boundless in exploring these wilds and green landscapes, some of which were off the beaten track as well.

Came a longer weekend, and we (MS, self, and another of our more talkative batch-mates) took off for a much-awaited sojourn across the Thekkadi Wildlife Reserve. Those were the days of State buses and no Uber cabs—so we boarded a roadworthy bus for Thekkadi. It was not a very long journey and we reached the location by sunset. The night was spent at a pre-booked forest guest house.

We were up at dawn and quickly changed into our jungle gear. While MS had on a pair of ankle-length Hunter boots, the rest of us were shod in basic sneakers and comfortable trousers. MS soon was ambling across to the entry edge of the vast foliage beckoning us into its abode. He (with his local lingo skills) also had managed to fix up a guide for our forthcoming trek inside this South Indian forest, known to harbour the larger mammals such as bears, elephants, and the occasional tiger too.

Off we went—our trio with the guide leading ahead, in a more or less single file. As we traversed through the tropical greens, the air got a bit more humid. The guide and MS, meanwhile, were chatting away in Malayalam. The rest two of us, not savvy with this Keralite mother tongue, tried to spot any of the forest fauna. A few Malabar giant squirrels with their huge bushy tails were espied, hopping away through the branches of tall trees on either side of our jungle trail.

As we moved in deeper into the glades, fragrant smells of exotic flower and plant species wafted ever so slowly into our nostrils. The guide had by now mingled back with our foot treads and even started explaining the layout of the huge Reserve.

I happened to notice that he was now constantly stamping his slipper-shod feet on the ground as he walked briskly with us. Espying nothing out of the ordinary except myriads of small twig-like forms on the trail path, I pushed that observation into the back of my mind.

Vague thoughts of some form of a mix of Kalaripayattu[1] and Mohiniattam[2] came up in my imagination, however.

We continued trying to now look for bears, some of which, as the guide informed, had been detected a few days back in this very patch of the forest. Although meeting a wild bear in its turf was pretty risky, our youthful enthusiasm was eager for more intense adventure.

After about three hours of our trek, the guide deviated a bit from the initial path and led us downhill to a small pool of water. This was a kind of watering hole for various animals and birds, and it was here that we sat down to have a bite, and stretch our legs.

---

1. An ancient Keralite martial arts form.
2. A classical dance form of Kerala.

The cool water was very inviting, and lo and behold, within less than a minute, I had unlaced my shoes and started taking off my cotton socks.

Then it happened—as I unrolled off my right leg sock, a very fat black worm-like thing dislodged itself from my instep skin! It was a leech, and in its wake it left a pretty big clotted round bruise on my foot.

As I bit on my sandwich, I had time to ruminate that I had done my bit to feed at least one of the Reserve's inhabitants. And MS finally informed me that all the guide's previous continuous feet stamping had been effected to dislodge any of the seemingly twig-like leeches from latching onto his mostly bare ankles or soles. Maybe the guide was one with the forest, or it had been not my day, but finally, blood had been drawn despite my fairly protected feet.

Anyway (as I pondered, ever the optimist), I had not needed the much-bandied salt treatment to get rid of the bloodsucker—so that was something.

I, of course, had not been sucker-punched by Ursidae but the very small and effective Hirudinae.

□

SSSSSLEEP!

The year-long Technical Courses for our batch of Sub Lts. had reached its halfway mark. We were ensconced in a scenic port of South India. Since we all belonged to the Executive branch of the Navy, the various subjects taught at various schools inside this Naval base—comprising Navigation, Communication and Weapons—were of utmost importance. They were after all, to form our bread and butter in the Naval years to come.

Now, we also had a short stint at the Seamanship School—essentially to learn the nuances of hull maintenance, various paint schemes on Naval vessels, and other associated topics. The coursework was far less rigorous than the conventional other Schools, but very important nevertheless. After all, as our Chief Instructor told us at the beginning that the Titanic had sunk basically because of substandard riveting in the underwater hull. So we, with all our youthful energy, dove straight into warping of hulls, ship stability equations[1] and imbibing the details of paint thinners and primers.

Anyway, it was a short week-long course, and the next door vista of the Naval jetties with a fantastic view of the adjoining sea channel swiped out any stress of the impending Assessment Tests on the weekend.

We had a very pleasant dispositioned Instructor M from Eastern India, who, apart from classroom instructions, also

1. These are the basis of equilibrium of a ship under various conditions of loading, list etc.

supervised our practical hands-on look at the mock-up rigs for hull maintenance and rope-work. Some of these outdoor periods used to happen in the afternoon session after lunch, amongst grumblings from the lazier lot of us, including myself (Sub Lt. SG).

One balmy afternoon, and we were (with some absentees) lined along a small pier, while M was putting his best in trying to perfect our understanding of the wood used in the construction of whalers. Long before drones regularly flew global skies, his voice, to my mind, was that, and more. As I tried to be attentive, I felt myself slipping into a semi-torpor, trying hard not to go into the full forty winks while standing upright!

'Yessssss SSS G", akin to Ka's hypnotic whisper in the *Jungle Book*, suddenly sounded near my ears.

M had slipped behind the class, sensing our languor. After all, he had a training session to complete. And his words had its desired effect—I was at least holding my eyes wide open for the rest of the half-hour period.

I could not admire M's presence of mind more-essentially his 'SSS's had replaced the ZZZZs!!

□

ASTERN STROKE!

Now, in the Navy, swimming is a much-required skill and is preferred across all ranks of the hierarchy. Naturally so, all command ports have Olympic-sized pools. These are mainly used for recreational swimming by Naval personnel and their families; they are also normally situated separately from the training pools used by the Naval diving fraternity.

I was then a young and somewhat wild Sub-Lieutenant posted for watch-keeping duties on a small ship based at one of our Naval commands. Being a fairly active person, I regularly frequented the swimming pool in the evenings for numerous and multi-stroke laps. I tried to do my swimming before the crowd hit the water. This was basically to maintain my lane without dashing or colliding with other swimmers, especially smaller children.

So there I was one fine evening, swimming along smoothly in an otherwise uncrowned pool, it being a weekend, wherein people had various other options for recreation—chief amongst which was the local club Saturday matinee show.

As I was switching my swimming strokes, I could espy some more people entering the pool. And amongst them was Commander C, who was well known for his deep professional knowledge, apart from his girth and copious drinking abilities. I pressed on regardless, focused on my smooth stroking motions through the water.

And then it suddenly happened! As I, backstroking, changed over after touching one end of the pool, I missed colliding with the huge bulk of Commander C, who was just getting warmed up with his breaststroke. As we passed each other like ships at sea, I heard his parting remark: "And what are you up to Subby-swimming forward with astern strokes, or swimming astern with forward engines?"

Long after this incident, we met several times. By this while, I had also mastered another motion—hovering and moving straight up in the air, as a HELO pilot.

Of course, we remembered each other even much after Commander C 'swallowed his anchor', especially when I was in the water using my favourite Astern Stroke!

□

WHAT'S IN A NAME!

We had two officers in the batch with the same name initials SS, and a common surname S. While one was a Bihari, the other could not be more different—a very tall Sikh. Some of our instructors in the initial training periods in the Navy confused the two names but once physically identified, did not make the same mistake again. We, of course, knew them to be as different as chalk and cheese.

Finally, after our Technical Courses, we bid adieu to each other and most of us got posted to different Naval ships for our watch-keeping phase. Some of us also applied for the aviation cadre and went directly to the Air Force Academy for flight training. All our training inputs over the past two years or so were to be now tested out at sea under the stringent and rigorous influence of Lord Varuna.

Some of us went to the bigger capital ships and some to the smaller vessels of the Navy. While the former afforded more complexity in ship systems, the smaller ships entailed more responsibilities due to a lesser on-board crew strength. This phase was to last anything from six months to a year.

Now, the two SSs were posted on different ships, based on opposite coasts. The Navy was then still paying us in cash (nowadays, of course, it is a fully computerised and finely managed system of pay in the bank). The end of the month saw us counting our valuable salary, and toting up expenses for the month. Since we were all mostly messed on-board, the outgo from our salary was generally predictable, although one odd person found himself borrowing a bit for clearing the drinks and cigarette bills. All in all, life was a breeze, and our salaries seemed to stretch quite a bit.

Now, one SS (on the Western coast Naval base) started getting considerably more salary than he used to be paid (the Navy used to send our pay slips separately but most of us rarely looked at them for reconciling our incomes). He was ecstatic, and forays to all the nice movie halls at Bombay became a regular outing for him. He shared his newfound 'hike' with us, and we wished him all the more. A few of us also thought of having a look at our pay slips to see if some more could be wangled out of the Naval Pay Office, sadly—with no luck.

After about three odd months of this largesse, suddenly SS (in Bombay of early 90s) did not get any salary for a particular month. Not very habituated to saving for a rainy day, he was dumbfounded and at a loss. Anyway, some of us bailed him out and he was only affected in his number of movie viewings (the on-board VCR also came to his rescue),

As things turned out, the Bombay SS had been getting a double package of salary and allowances—including those actually due to the other coast Command SS, whereas, the beleaguered other SS was all at sea regarding his 'missing' part of the salary.

Finally, when the Pay Office realised the error, they deducted the extra amount from the 'wealthier' SS, over a single month.

Later on, the Bombay SS became an ace Naval Aviator and the other a fine Logistics Officer.

The Navy had also exposed us to a 'Doppelganger'-event with a twist!

□

GOOD COMPANY!

I had just completed my Mids time on a recently commissioned Capital Ship of the Navy. The next appointment placed me on the opposite coast with the other big fleet of the Navy. I had been now appointed on-board one of the oldest missile frigates of the Navy for obtaining my watch-keeping ticket.

This ship was operational, with fairly vintage sensors and functional gunnery systems. I had joined just before the peak summer season-and had settled in with an upper berth in a multiple-bunked cabin along with a few Sub Lts. of slightly higher seniority. As expected on older ships, we had our quota of rats to share our cabin with, and the odd worn-out deck tiles to contend with. However, the ship was fully sailing worthy, and that was most important—for sailings meant much sought-after sea experience, and an earlier watch-keeping qualification.

It was around May, and our base port was experiencing its usual showers as the monsoon kicked in. Soon enough, we were tasked with a sortie (my first on this ship) off Madras (now Chennai). Also, we had to tag along in company with another newer and larger Destroyer of our Fleet. I was assisting the Navigator, who instructed me to man the Radar Room during entering and leaving harbour evolutions.

We sailed out one fine morning (or it seemed 'fine' enough at first), casting off in succession after the Destroyer ahead of us. I had plonked myself in the Radar Room and was getting briefed by the Navigator's Yeoman (a grizzled veteran sailor) regarding the various controls of the all-important Navigation Radar.

As we untethered from our berth and eased out into the Harbour Channel, I could feel the swell in the water and the more than normal rock-and-roll motion of our ship. Anyway, as I reminded myself, this was seamanship and navigation for real, and I needed to guide the bridge as efficiently and correctly as possible. And, boy was I to be tested that day!

The ship's speed was slower than we were habituated to, as we traversed out through the various turns in the Channel out into the open Bay of Bengal. Suddenly, the 'Blind'[1] was much in demand. The Navigator made the warning announcement for stormy weather and squall ahead, and I grappled with my 'Blind Pilotage' notebook and pencil as the Ship heeled one side and then the other in a frighteningly regular manner.

Since bad things also sometimes come in packages, I soon enough realised that the Radar Index Error was greater than the width of the Channel at numerous points!

Anyway, our Radar Room reports were somewhat correlated and collated by the Navigator (a veteran who has since risen to a Vice Admiral rank), and the ship safely exited the otherwise well-marked Channel out into the expanse of the rough seas. Meanwhile, all efforts to follow the senior Destroyer in the company had been discarded (In fact, as I came to know later, we had been told during halfway through the Channel to act independently to manoeuvre our ship safely and securely.).

It was stormy weather throughout and we just missed the cyclone, which had passed very near to Madras (now Chennai) just before our reaching near the same port. There, we could retrieve the lost anchor and cable of a Coast Guard Ship, which had tried to weather the cyclone through staying anchored outside the port limits of Madras.

1. Naval fleet ships can also operate in company of each other.

As we returned to homeport (again independent of our Senior Naval Ship), with me on the 'Blind' chair, an inspection of the ship's compartments revealed significant damage to the aft Quarterdeck Sailors' Messes—a lot of deck tiles had disappeared along with apparel, shoes and sundry items washed out into the deep depths of the sea.

As we tied back at our familiar berth, the first thing I did was to invite my batch-mate from the Senior Ship (an aviator who had just been transferred from our Ship to the Destroyer recently) for a much-needed drink.

After all the adventures, we admittedly missed each other's 'company' these past few days at sea!

□

DIVING NOW DIVING NOW!

We were now firmly entrenched in our classroom, sports and regular Assessment Exams routine at our Submarine Training School. The eleven of us were boarded and lodged at the attached Officers Wardroom Mess located within the Base campus. We were now also being groomed for the all-important and mandatory sunk /disabled submarine Escape Drills. This was being done under the watchful eyes of an extremely professional and dynamic CDO-Lt T.

Our recently appointed Officer-in-Charge at the Training School, Commander A had joined the School after relinquishing Command of a frontline submarine of the Navy. Known as a stickler for discipline and cleanliness, he was also regular in his berating of mostly everyone for low efficiency and being 'not up to the mark'. But he was also very straightforward and forthright and one felt whatever he ticked people off for, he rarely kept a grudge against anyone.

One fine afternoon, and we had all gathered at the Wardroom Bar for Pre-lunch Drinks[1] (PLD) to bid farewell to an officer from the Instructor Staff. It was a balmy and pretty hot Saturday, and the cool AC inside the bar lifted both kinds of spirits. Much beer flowed in the traditional shining white-metalled tankards (which had a mirrored glass bottom for the mythical King's 'shilling"). It was considered rude to ask the

1. Traditionally drinks are served in the Wardroom bar prior to lunch, for occasions of officers' promotions, bidding adieu to an outgoing officer etc.

guest to stop drinking, and he being one of the champs of beer drinking, the wine steward had a tough time calling up all his stock to keep us 'liquefied'.

After about an hour and a half, we were (the junior most around) now getting a bit anxious, since the dining mess was about to close and our growling stomachs (mostly laced with copious amounts of only the brownish-yellow lager and some small eats[1]) were sounding fairly ominous. Anyway, we had to stick on, especially since the guest was around. Commander A was enjoying his beer and having an animated chat with Lt T—the Escape Training School CDO.

Even as some of us were drifting towards the sofas to plonk down (generally PLDs entail having drinks and snacks and mingling around in a standing position), we were suddenly attentive to an argumentative exchange emanating from the bar counter area. The Commander and Lt. T had fairly squared off against each other—facing one to one with variously filled tankards.

"Sir, I have on record a dive to 35 metres—plan to exceed that soon", quipped the CDO T.

"That's nothing T, I have dived to 250 metres many times", said the ex-sub Captain.

We could also find the Commander gesticulating with his hands trying to stress his point and further probably (as gathered from conversation snatches, which we picked up) discussing the inherent risks of submarining versus clearance diving. He seemed to be just warming up; and we were fairly reconciled that the biggest risk that day was that we would miss our lunch, whether or not the 'sub dived even deeper'.

It was then that our guest, a 'bundle man'[2], finished his last drink of the day. The Training Commander, ever the regulations follower, thereafter closed the proceedings after

1. Snacks served with drinks.
2. A married Naval officer or a sailor staying in family Quarters.

asking for last drinks, if any. The steward wound up the bar, and soon we all strode outside.

And, oh yes, the kindly dining hall Chief Steward had kept the door open so our appetites were satiated, after all, that afternoon long ago.

I had an early naval experience that day as to what 'in the drink' could entail!

□

MONEY, MONEY, MONEY!

I was undergoing a Basic Submarines Training at the Navy's scenic Base port in South India. Nestled between hills on one side and one of the Navy's largest ports, the large campus provided enough space for various sports, a large Parade Ground-cum-HELO Landing Pad, and a well-stocked library, apart from being the alma mater for all submariners past and present. Our routine was the usual Classroom sessions in the forenoon, followed by sports in the evenings and occasional forays on-board submarine for the practical initiation into this most secretive and potent arm of any Navy. All in all, a very satisfying tenure, especially for book lovers like me, and I caught up with a lot of my favourites from the library.

Now, we were a youthful lot in the early twenties, and had lots of time to engage in other activities like an occasional squash game with the Captain of the Base (he had a favourite advice to give—he had paid for using the courts at Sweden from where he had just returned after an Attache tenure, and thus exhorted us to use the free sports facilities available at our Naval courts). The two of us also used to frequent the nearby sailing club where-horrors, once we managed to upend an Enterprise-class sailing boat (which is another story to tell).

Halfway through the course, wherein quite a few of us had also managed to flunk a few subjects, the three of us were feeling the ennui of a too staid life (especially after our previous short stints on various afloat ships with their never-a-dull-moment experiences). But just as we were ruing our 'drab' lives, like the saying about man proposing and God disposing, a once-in-a-lifetime event came our way.

The Naval Command based at the port city was planning a grand series of adventure activities to commemorate and start the customary Navy Week. Our Submarine Training Base was the overall administrative and funding authority for these events. The high point of the events jamboree was a two-week-long trip on a rubber motorised Gemini down around 1500 km of the longest river in South India. And we were at the right tipping point to volunteer for this adventure—our Training Officer's discomfiture (after all we would miss around a month's crucial training programme) notwithstanding!

So the three of us got right into the fray of things. Two of us were being selected to survey the river all along its nearly full length, and the rest two to arrange items like the Gemini and its accessories, such as purchasing specific logo branded T-Shirt and Denim Shorts for our eight-strong crew, etc. I was also entrusted with the responsibility of the Logistician and Accounting Officer for the whole trip (we had to, of course, put up a statement of accounts after the trip, for an audit of the use of Command funds). So, it was that I started carrying a register from Day 1, to endorse and keep track of all income and expenses.

After the nearly two-week-long survey, we booked our rail tickets for the travel to our starting point in the hilly regions of Maharashtra, from where the river started its upper course. Our adventure started right away since we had not got reserved seats at such short notice, we had to travel in the freight bogie of the train for one part of our journey. All this was grist for the mill, as we soon ticked off various pre-river trip events like the traditional Puja at the starting spot (this is also a Hindu holy spot with a famous and pretty old temple), meeting with various state officials and last-minute tying-up with the onshore organisers, who had been with us throughout our planning stage.

Finally, as we lowered our inflated Gemini in the cool and crystal-clear river waters, and cast off, did realisation dawn that we were totally on our own. We were to have no communication with our shore supporters for the next fifteen days or so until we reached the culmination point after crossing nearly the full expanse of two of the largest south Indian states.

The total experience was unforgettable (more of that in my next book)—but one of the highly vexing points in my kitty was the exorbitant price of petrol we were paying en route (the fuel was a must for our guzzler of the Gemini OBM).

It was only later that we came to know that a particular government policy had banned the sale of petrol in cans, only allowing fuel filling directly into tanks of vehicles! What this policy did for us was that we were mostly buying the precious stuff at black market prices from various en route onshore pumps as we meandered our watery way! The net result was occasional rationed food and exhausting our money bags (not that we had much, in any case).

When we finally entered the backwaters of our destination near the sea on the East coast, I, the great Logistician, had only a 10 paise[1] coin in my pocket.

As I spent the next two weeks or so trying to account for the spent funds (with mostly scraps of various illegible and wet smudged receipts to go by), I had this momentous and ironical epiphany that-

The dead (petrol from extinct reptiles) had cost us far more than the alive (our living expenses)!

□

1. A very small denomination of Indian currency coin, no longer in use, 100 paise =1 rupee.

BLUE MOON!

The Navy had recently set up several coastal detachments down south along the Eastern shores of the country. They were staffed with an average of three officers and a retinue of junior and senior sailors. A mix of permanent EEC[1] structures and large-sized tents accommodated the personnel manning most of these detachments; both fresh and dry rations were supplied from the nearest Naval Base. The sight of the monthly ration truck with its Petty Officer-in-Charge standing atop its roof (a la Amitabh Bachchan), arriving to deliver volumes of rations cheered us like nothing else. Rum (the sailor drink of yore) quotas were also issued regularly and movies screened occasionally to keep ennui from setting in.

Life on our one such detachment was pretty routine—our work involved lots of administrative work (such as rations accounting, maintaining discipline, regular coastal patrols on hired fishing trawlers, etc.). Many a weekend was spent enjoying beers and snacks at other nearby detachments on various personnel's birthdays. The fresh fish and other seafood delivered by the weekly vendor added to the culinary experience of our thoroughly professional Naval Cooks. For me (a Bengali), the menu was like manna from heaven.

A few odd disciplinary issues came up but were generally tackled in an all-pulling in the same direction manner.

Now, the detachment had sailor staff from diverse units of the Naval Commands. The Navy being far more equipment

1. European Economic Community.

and less manpower-intensive, the detachments had more than their share of medically downgraded personnel, who only could be spared, especially from leanly staffed ships. However, this was more than made up by the zeal and dynamism of the senior sailors, especially the Petty Officers (who usually form the best and most hardworking crew and in-charges on ships too). They ensured correct routines, regular weapons training, checking various rigs of the junior lot and smoothening any potential conflict events.

Petty Officer MS was a Gunnery specialist and one of the brightest of the lot. Ever enthusiastic in sports, weapons practices and ensuring the boat patrol routines, his energy levels were legion. A regular-rum-drinker, he regaled us all with his own sea experience tales time and again.

So, it was a great surprise to me (I was also responsible for discipline enforcement at the place) when I was informed by the Master-Chief-in-Arms one fine day that MS had been involved in an ugly fracas the night before with another Chief Petty Officer at the detachment. Now this was serious stuff especially since it involved the senior lot. Anyway, I decided to first have an informal chat with the aggrieved Chief Petty Officer before going on to the defaulter table, which followed such incidents.

CPO SS was summoned and as he elaborated, PO MS had come back from outside liberty, swaying punch-drunk through the Security Gates well late into the previous night. The CPO, who was the Duty Chief that night, accosted him and asked him his reasons for late-coming. MS immediately started attacking him verbally and they nearly came to blows. The CPO also related that they had had ego issues even during MS's training days when SS had been his Instructor In-Charge. Finally, SS had to manhandle the drunken MS and tie him to a chair overnight to prevent further escalation of the matter!

I recounted the incident to the OIC Detachment, essentially

preparing for the decision to be meted out at the Defaulters Table. But what our OIC added furthermore was even more out of the blue!

There had been multiple incidents over the past few months when PO MS had behaved strangely and abnormally with various other staff—and these had all happened on full moon nights! And yes-the present altercation with the CPO had also happened on a *Poornima*[1]!

A judicious decision was thence taken to award stoppage of liberty (a relatively lighter punishment) for some days to MS, in spite of SS baying for his blood.

The Navy also offered me the rare once-in-a-blue moon experience of an incident, recalling the Bard in 'Othello' –

"It is the very error of the moon.
She comes more near the earth
than she was wont. And makes
men mad".

□

1. Hindi word for the full moon.

STRAIGHTENED

I was doing my naval Divers' Training course at a picturesque southern port of India. The routine was pretty tough with lots of extremely strenuous physical exercises daily. Apart from these, we also needed to attend regular classroom instructions to understand and imbibe the nuances of the bio-physics behind operating in the highly unconventional environment of the sea and ocean depths.

Now, mostly our days started with an early morning 10 km run on the road circumscribing our Naval Base. Our instructors (all sailors from the Diving cadre) ran close alongside us. They ensured we did not slacken off since these exercises were meant to toughen us for the upcoming rigours of actual diving evolutions under the saline Arabian Sea backwaters, which ran along a channel skirting the Naval Base and thereon towards civilian areas.

After we settled down into our schedule, we started off our initial dives within a customised tank, installed at the Diving School. Most of us could now independently wear our highly specialised diving bodysuits and don the fairly heavy and crucial breathing equipment and accessories.

One fine morning, our Senior Diving Instructor led us on a jog to a nearby road-cum-rail bridge. We were togged up in our neoprene suits and boots while lugging our diving equipment including air cylinders on our backs. As we neared the climb from the straight road onto the bridge, a single thought flashed in our minds: "This is it, our first dives into the fast-flowing channel seawater depths below."

The Senior Instructor, called Chief Sa'ab by us, gave precise and business-like instructions on the exact evolution to be followed. His list of don'ts (which could make the difference between life and death in the greyish-green water) especially pricked up my ears. Of particular note was the cautionary regarding notorious jellyfishes, which also shared these waters. After all, many an unwary diver had experienced painful stings from these seemingly lightweight cnidarians.

However, all of us were agog with excitement and enthusiasm. The first rubicon would be crossed today—from the waveless diving tank minus stinging tentacles to the not-so-clear and fast current flow of the backwaters, with its natural denizens.

I was third in line, and after a wait of about 5 minutes when the first two divers jumped off, it was me on the bridge edge. After a last-hand motion to tighten my face mask, I counted to three and jumped off, flippered feet pointing downwards as straight as possible.

Events unfolded smoothly thereafter—the splashdown, alignment with the current, speedy swimming through the seawater and the completion at the earmarked jetty within our Naval Base. And no stings for any of us, which was a huge saving grace.

Finally, all of us trainees wound up the session for the day—taking off our flippers and tethered breathing apparatus. As I let the tension creep out of my body, I was a bit perplexed when the Senior Diving Instructor (who was discussing something with his team of diver sailors some way off) sent word for me.

I quickly scrambled up from my sitting position and jogged towards him, still clad in the bodysuit. He took me a bit aside and informed me that I had done okay, but for my initial jump. This jump, he explained, was not done with a straight body, as he had explicitly told us in his directives. Even as I protested, claiming rightfully that I had been the diving and swimming champ at my training in the Defence Academy before starting in the Navy, I could make out his disagreement with my defence.

Finally, after about two minutes of this discussion between young blood and sobered experiences, he gave me this gem of advice (one which is true of the vicissitudes of life too):

"Lt M Sahab, streyt maney tedda aur tedda maney streyt...." [1]

□

1 Translated it means 'straight means curved and curved means straight'.

BRIDGEMAN-SHIP!

I was posted as a Watchkeeping Lt. on one of the Navy's frontline diesel-electric subs. I, along with a batchmate of mine, were used to the 'boat-hopping' for sailing on different submarines of the same class (which had a smaller crew and frequently required to fill their officers' complement due to leave absences of the appointed staff). Both of us were bachelors staying at the nearby Naval Officers Mess, and life was quite carefree; also, we were at a vital learning stage of our service, in this most potent and risky of naval branches.

Now, the Navy also had a mother ship for catering to logistical, power supply, ordnance replenishment, etc., for its submarines. This capital ship was fairly old and equipped with vintage sensors. But it was customary to sail it for first check dives of recently refitted boats, and a fairly senior Captain commanded this only vessel of its kind in our Navy.

One such sortie required a junior submarine branch officer on board the ship, as an advisor to guide the Captain. And I was the chosen one. Came the day, and I boarded the ship.

As I was deciding where to plonk myself, I was apprised by the EXO that the Captain required me on the bridge, even as the ship cast off from Bombay (now Mumbai). I knew that the Captain was a Dolphin branded officer, and known for his tough and demanding professionalism from junior officers. So, it was with some trepidation that I made my way up the catwalk and onto the ladder reaching the Bridge.

The Bridge was quite large, and I added myself to the

Navigator, the EXO and of course the Old Man on his chair. The ship cast off and made underway smoothly, and soon we were leaving the limits of the port and into the Arabian Sea's frothy waves (it was around October and rains had long receded—so the swell and roll was comfortable).

The Navigator handed over to the ASWO of the ship for the forenoon watch. The quizzing and the grilling by the Captain then began in right earnest. And most of his queries were sub-related. The ASWO, seemingly a greenhorn, looked well uncomfortable, but there was to be no escape. Meanwhile, I was still there as I had been for the past two hours (the old man had not probably realised my presence) quite bored by now, and was contemplating whether to interfere in this 'buzzer round Q&A' session, to mark my existence.

"Lt G, you are from those boats that require a PCT, right?' suddenly came the aimed query in my direction. As I answered in the affirmative with a visible straightening up, I could make out the Captain's chair swivelling in my direction. "Pray tell me then, what is the rating of the main motor of the boat?" came the next. This was my lucky break since the recently concluded PCT-OJT Board had had us all rote-memorising this kind of information. As I rattled out a crisp and precise answer, the Captain gave a soft "OK", and immediately requested the EXO (who was around as well), to allot me comfortable quarters on the ship during the six days sortie.

I was given a double-bunked cabin all to myself with a dedicated AC unit (on Russian class ships such as these, a 'private' AC unit is a luxury). Now, I needed to kill time because, from the Bridge meeting, it was evident I was now a sort of 'guest' on-board, with vital advice given correctly to the ship's Captain. So I meandered towards the Wardroom and hit jackpot. It was around 7 pm, and there were three others in the Wardroom—the ship's EO, LO and a Medical Officer who had also embarked to provide medical cover to submarine crew, if so required.

We hit it off immediately and soon started an animated Bridge game. The days rolled by, and as the sky and horizon outside grew darker and starlit together, our Bridge sessions continued into the nights. Meanwhile, the ship ponderously made her way to Goa—her port of stopover during the sortie.

Our Bridge sessions continued on a nightly routine (the EO and LO in any case, had to be especially more vigilant and be around at night times, considering the age of on-board machines and various systems). They both also frequently attended various Duty Officers' nightly reports and gave directives from the Ward Intercom, if warranted. Copious amounts of the wonderful coffee made by a very efficient steward fuelled our dark-hour Bridging. All in all, it was a memorable sojourn, made sweeter by our sunny Goa stay.

The gap between a professional Bridge and the card game of the same name was bridged in those days.!

□

Section-4

BLOW BALLAST!

Our newly commissioned submarine needed to be degaussed, facilities for which were available in a naval port on the opposite coast. So, we set sail for a good 45-day sortie (15 out of which were to be spent at the Degaussing Basin).

With a brief stopover enroute at a port (where we replenished our rations and other stores), we entered our destination port of call, where we were warmly welcomed by Command officials. We were towed into the Degaussing Basin where the sub was tethered with a set of super-strong rope hawsers in the middle of the Basin. Then various thick cables were laid around the hull for relevant measurements.

That evening, we also attended a grand evening reception party at the nearby Command Officer's Mess. All of us officers were also provided boarding and lodging for the duration of our port stay, at the same mess.

Now, from the sub to the adjoining jetty, there was a distance of about 200 metres. The only transport for covering this distance through the seawater was a plastic tub-like vessel, which was capable of accommodating about five people at any time. This 'boat' did not have any propulsion means, and one of us had to stand up inside the vessel, grip one of the tethering hawsers and pull towards the sub. So, we got habituated to using this 'boat' in shifts to arrive on-board and depart punctually every day during working hours.

One day, a new officer Lt K was to report for his training

sea sortie on-board our submarine. It was early in the morning and four of us had already boarded the 'boat' when along came Lt S, huffing and puffing. Quite stocky and round, he requested us to bring the 'boat' closer to the jetty. Before we knew what happened, he jumped onto the 'boat'.

'Wham'—the 'boat' tilted and then turned turtle. All of us fell overboard into the water, with one of the dockyard workers hanging onto the hawser for dear life (he was a non-swimmer). After we got some seawater inside us and ruined our uniforms, we could upright the 'boat', and after boarding, it, arrived on the sub in a bedraggled state, Lt S included.

I immediately christened Lt K as ' BALLAST', and unofficially declared him 'trained'—for who could ' dive' a boat better than such an expert submariner!

□

LET FLY!

Submarining is a rigorous and at times tedious life; operating from one extreme of nearly 15-16 hours of sleeping when dived (to conserve on oxygen levels and reduce carbon dioxide levels) to the other of intense four-five hours action at dead of night in the combat centre, whilst tracking 'enemy' ships when exercising with the Fleet. Even though physics and the inky blue sea depths mostly favoured the sub, we submariners could not let our guard down ever, due to the inherently risky nature of operating at significantly great ocean depths for long periods.

I was borne aboard the latest diesel-electric submarine of the Navy. Yet to gain a specific specialisation, I, along with a course mate, were the do-it-all of the boat. From Navigation to Communication to Weapons firing to even Machinery Room rounds, we could be rotated amongst any department. The boat was also recently out of an extended refit[1] schedule, and for the Command HQ, we were a potent 'sword arm', with lots of sea sorties on our plate.

After a fairly long two-week outing, we were returning to our Base port of Bombay. En route, we had had a successful practice torpedo firing exercise with the might of the Surface Navy. Since I was carrying out the role of Assistant Weapons Officer, I was naturally feeling quite pleased with my responsible performance on the FCS for the torpedo shoot.

Early in the morning on the day of our ETA at Bombay, I

1. A refit schedule for longer duration.

was on watch on the Bridge of our surfaced boat. The Captain came up for his breath of fresh air (after being cooped up inside our dived sub for nearly twelve days without sunlight) and his routine smoke (although a fairly regular cigarette smoker, he rarely had a chance for even a few puffs whilst in a dived state). We had got the Captain's chair rigged up (only he had this privilege on the boat, of sitting whilst on Bridge). Comfortable with his cigarette and waiting for his early morning black coffee (the steward was on the way up with that soon), he had a look at the horizon through his binoculars, and then the casing for any damages (which included paint peels or even a damaged 'proud' sonar transducer, though that event was very rare).

It was then that I remembered that we had not yet discharged the SSE loaded in the forward ejector (this had been loaded during the weapons firing program the previous day).

Upon my informing and reminding him, he (who was also incidentally a weapons specialist), coolly asked me to ready the torpedo room (the forward launcher[1] was operated by the torpedo crew) for firing off the yellow SSE cartridge. Funnily, I had been under a mistaken impression that the SSEs should be discharged only in a dived boat, and the anticipation of seeing an SSE ejected, whist on a surfaced boat, really excited my curiosity.

After giving the necessary orders to the torpedo crew, we waited for the few minutes it took to prepare the launcher tube for firing the SSE cartridge. This was a once-in-a lifetime event for me, and I felt blessed that I would be probably one of the very few spectators to this pyrotechnics launch from a surfaced sub.

"Fire forward SSE" came the crisp Captain's order, and I repeated the same on the intercom to torpedo room. After the

1The metal tube inside the submarine which is used to fire the SSE.

acknowledgment came that the tube had been fired, there was a brief lull that I feared was a misfire. But no—it was not! With a sound of around 50 Diwali[1] firework rockets going off, the SSE cartridge shot up from its launcher, nearly scraped the side of the Bridge (the sub's sail[2]) less than a foot from both of us, and flew towards the aft of the submarine. It thereafter soared ever higher in the sky before it hit water amongst a cloud of yellow smoke.

It was all so sudden, the Captain nearly stumbled off his chair and I ducked automatically! 'That was CLOSE" said the soft-spoken and otherwise nonchalant Captain.

I mentally noted the very rare event of an 'Ejection Seat' operation on a submarine Bridge, that day!

□

1. A major festival of lights in India.
2. The raised portion of a submarine, wherein the upper lid opens.

NEARLY MISSED THE WORLD!

I was a carefree Sub Lt. then, posted on a recently commissioned sub. I was boarded and lodged at the sprawling Command Officers Mess, right next to the Arabian Sea shoreline. The lodging was in a two-room apartment with an integral bathroom. Food services were facilitated at the in-house dining hall.

Weekends, or whenever I had an off day (which were quite infrequent since we sailed a lot, and many a day was also spent on-board for OOD duties), were spent in catching up on sleep. Evening walks along the seaside walkway (these adjoined the lawns of the mess) and occasional badminton games were enough for keeping fit at a fairly youthful age. Quite a few evenings were also spent in the company of course mates over drinks and dinner, at the adjacent club or in the excellent mess bar.

All in all, life was a breeze, matching the cool sea winds which were unmatched for their calming and soporific value.

Now, the Command Mess had a neatly manicured lawn with a balustrade opening from the main central foyer. A *kuchcha*[1] track led from the lawn to the concrete seaside walkway. The lawn was the main venue for many evening receptions and even the ubiquitous annual Navy Ball. The Ball was also an occasion for the crowning of the Navy Queen every year, which was a pretty tough contest with plenty of glamour models and starlets vying for the coveted tiara.

It was the 90s, and India had had several Miss Worlds and

1. Unmetalled track or road.

Miss Universes on the global stage. Also, the selection round for the final list of Navy Queen contestants was slated before the Ball in December. And the venue for this event was the Mess lawn, with the previous year's Miss World as the chief judge and guest of the Navy.

We came to know that the tickets for the event were on sale, but for some strange reason, they were only meant for non in-living officers of the Mess! Our entreaties to the Mess Secretary (otherwise an empathetic and generous person) for our share of entry tickets, fell on deaf ears.

Determined and schooled in tackling various hard knocks, a few of us like-minded mess denizens resolved to attend or view the event, come what may.

Came the 'event' on a Saturday, and we had all managed to wangle our ways out of OOD duties. First step taken—we started our preparations on a war footing. I fished out a pair of binoculars, Sub Lt. D arranged for some groundsheets while N handled drinks for all of us.

Up we went—right to the rooftop of our apartment building (normally none of us ever ventured here). And as imagined, we had an excellent view of the lawn down below, from alongside the rooftop parapet. Here we set up our post on groundsheets—akin to US forces taking up sniper positions in Iraq!

As the first of hosts arrived for the red carpet event and the Navy band struck up a fine near-operatic tune, N passed around the first of our many drinks along with the eatables. I adjusted the binoculars' focus and marvelled at the clarity of the view on display. Even as we espied Irina Skliva (the preceding year's Miss World) sashaying to a rousing welcome and introduction to the top brass and eager Navy Queen candidates—I mused out loud:

"Would not miss this for the World....!"

□

FIRE CONTROL!

Submariners, or at least most of them, are a quirky lot. Whether they join this risk-prone Naval arm because they are unconventional or they develop their 'habits' due to long hours being shut off from the outside world in a steel tube, could be a matter for animated debate. Even military doctors have tried to figure out the clinical and maybe psychological changes associated with these underwater stays. How much of these actual study results affect the sub crew themselves, could be conjectural at best.

Nowhere was this 'quirkiness' more evident than during my experience while as EXO of a diesel-electric boat. We had a strict taskmaster of a Captain, who was also very caring and loyal towards each member of the crew. We were serving on-board the Navy's Russian Foxtrot class submarines (now remembered with fond nostalgia only). My departmental officers also included some borne as unspecialised Watch-keeping Officers. These officers were continually rotated amongst the Navigation, Sonar, Torpedo and Communication sub-departments to enable work amalgamation and affect a well-rounded training before they went off for their specialist courses.

One such officer—Lt. I—had recently been inducted into the Torpedo department and was now an integral part of the forward Torpedo Room denizens during Practice Torpedo shoots. He was under the ASWO's tutelage, and I quizzed him occasionally to have a feedback about his imbibing of practical on-board knowledge regarding the diverse systems moulded into the all-important 'business end' of the boat.

We had decided to finally have a practice firing, wherein Lt. I was to be the de facto conducting and implementing Officer right from preparation of the Torpedo tubes till the actual firing and discharge of the 'fish[1]'. Accordingly, we carried out attack manoeuvres[2] for detection, tracking and final calculations for launching the 'fish' on the target ship (a surface Naval capital ship of our fleet).

All was ready at the Control Room end; we had matched bearings, and waiting for the Captain's final order. 'Fire Torpedo Tube 2' came his rasping voice, and I repeated the directive on the intercom to Torpedo Room. A minute passed while we waited for the acknowledgment and feedback that the 'Tube No. 2' had been fired. But as the moments ticked by, there was only silence from the forward end of the sub!

As I (by now adapted to the Captain's volcanic temperament and impatience with professional errors) looked at the stopwatch, I came to a quick decision. Picking up the Intercom and switching to the Main Broadcast setting (in case the torpedo crew had not heard the first time order for firing), I said in a louder voice: "Fire Torpedo Tube No. 2."

Immediately came a strident and fairly alarmed voice of Lt. I: "Fire, fire, fire.....Fire in Torpedo Room!" As the Captain and others in the Control Room looked at me with growing apprehension, I ran towards the forward side and into the Torpedo Room.

The compartment was spick and span, the PO In-charge of torpedo crew was standing by to pull the local firing trigger, and Lt I was looking sheepish and a bit dazed. Yes, as he explained softly, he had dozed off (he had had the graveyard

1. Refers to the torpedo.
2. Various changes of course and speed to achieve consistent tracking and firing on the designated target.

watch the previous night), and when prodded by my second order from Control Room, had only heard the word 'Fire..." with cognition.

Anyway, the 'fire' was put out (including the about-to-flame-out Captain's temper), and we redid the whole exercise for a near-perfect shoot.

Lt. I got his first lesson that day that FIRE is both friend and enemy to a submariner!

□

DOWN THE HATCH!

Our recently commissioned Naval submarine was undergoing a Short Refit[1] during the summer months at base port before we resumed our undersea vigil. Although we could now follow a fairly easier harbour routine, numerous occasions had us extending our working hours due to vital on-board work by the repairing dockyard staff. However, this was grist for the mill, since the final aim was to get the boat back into tiptop sail-worthy condition.

The Captain had taken a much-needed vacation, and the EXO was officiating in his absence. I was appointed as the Weapons Officer and had my fair share of workload for getting the torpedo tubes cleared by the Inspecting Authority for the upcoming firing season. We also followed a 1-in-3 roster for harbour OOD duties.

One fine Monday, and we received orders that since the top-level political establishment had changed guard, the new 'Ministerial Committee would be visiting our sub in the harbour in a week, for a walk around. Now, this was VVIP stuff, and under the EXO's tutelage, we got around to make the sub shipshape for the visit. This included cleaning up the sub interiors, painting up equipment, wherever possible, and, of course, a full coat of paint on the outside hull surface. Staff sailors were dispatched to thc Dockyard Paint Shop and other subs to get the much vital cans of paint, while dockyard staff had to be liasoned with, to 'close up' as many machinery

1. A refit of around three months.

as possible to further refine the interior compartments' appearance.

All was going like clockwork when just two days before the dignitaries were to embark on board, the EXO informed us that the Committee Head was on the stockier and well-fed side. We were also informed that the dignitary was not much comfortable with ladders and climbing up sloping gangplanks. Minds were put together and it was the venerable EXO himself who suggested soft-soled slip-on shoes for use of the honourable committee head. Accordingly, I immediately visited the nearest Bata[1] shoe store and could manage to get the shoes. For good measure, two pairs of successive sizes were bought. These were to be kept ready near the Trot's table on the forward casing, just before the visit.

Came the day, and we had been shifted by tugs to a far cleaner jetty and had a freshly painted pontoon between the sub and the jetty. New ropes had been used to tether the boat, and as the EXO and I (the OOD) slowly walked on the jetty from forward till aft end of the sub, we could not but help admiring our fine-looking and potent Naval vessel.

Soon enough, a flurry of Staff vehicles came up towards our berth. I ensured the gangway staff was shipshape and ready with their customary bugle and pipes to receive the VVIP, who was escorted by the Chief of Naval Staff. A sailor was standing with the slip-on shoes next to the jetty edge of the fairly long and steeply inclined gangplank. The dignitary was offered the shoes as planned, and after replacing his footwear with the soft-soled ones, he climbed onto the gangplank and made his way towards the sub end.

Customary Naval pipes and salutes being done with, the EXO took over (with me a step behind), leading the retinue of around seven officials for a short walk around the casing and a brief history about our boat. Next, the VVIP had to enter

1. One of the most popular shoes brand in India.

the innards of the sub through an open hatch, located at the forward end.

As the dignitary neared the hatch, I realised with slowly growing trepidation that he would not make it inside easily due to a rotund girth. And we had not accounted for this variable at all!

The ever quick-thinking EXO had already grasped this portent and beckoned me to his side even as the VVIP took his first step on the around six-foot ladder leading from the hatch to the Torpedo Room. With an ease belying the sensitiveness of the issue (I was however on pins and needles), the EXO and I gently and firmly grasped the shoulders of the VVIP visitor, and pressed down.

My torpedo loading experience (wherein torpedoes have to be pushed into their tubes having very minimal internal side clearances) was put to test! Everybody (including the CNS, who was still now a mute spectator) around heaved sighs of relief as the dignitary touched the Torpedo Room deck tiles.

The visit, all in all, was a resounding success, and the extra pair of slip-on soft-soled shoes were kept on board for later use if required.

In retrospect, the day gave a highly unconventional twist to the adage—'Down the Hatch'!

□

SWEET WATER NECTAR!

We were borne on a diesel-electric submarine of the Navy, which had recently been commissioned, and was fully deep into its operational cycle. Nearly every fleet exercise had us sailing off for various Coordinated Anti-submarine exercises, practice torpedo shoots (both as target and firing submarine roles), patrolling in shallow waters, etc.

One such sea sortie was a longish one, which involved us stopping over at two ports en route. The second port of call was the verdant green Cochin (Kochi) with its beckoning coconut palms and Chinese fishing nets lining the shore alongside the port entrance channel. The layover was a full three days—enough to enable each duty watch to have a day off for shore liberty. And the fairly long and busy dived passage from our base port had further incentivised us to consider the languorous backwaters of this South Indian port, as a sight for sore eyes.

With the sub tied up alongside the jetty in the neat and scenic Naval harbour, the EXO announced the routine for the next few days. Soon, the first batch of Liberty men peeled off for their dose of terra firma and gorging on seafood (Kochi is a haven for exotic seafood like lobsters and choice seawater fish).

I was on duty on-board as the Assistant OOD (this was also a training sortie for me to get my OOD and OOW tickets), and was soon on the casing, checking for strains on the rope (Kochi is notorious for its intense tidal level changes—thus stressing the berthing hawsers). I was also keeping an eye out for any senior officers planning to step on-board (the fleet ships had also entered the harbour before us and most surface ship COs were senior to our Captain). The EXO, who was also the OOD, had, meanwhile, a break to freshen up inside the boat.

Sometime in the evening (there was still light in the skies above), I suddenly saw a senior ranked submarine branch officer Commodore S, on the jetty alongside. Within no time he had beckoned me, and I (after informing the EXO) hurried onto the gangway and across to the jetty. As it transpired, the said officer handed me a biggish sack, instructing me that these were freshly plucked tender coconuts, which he would collect once we reached Bombay some days later. I saluted, collected the goodies, and made my way back. Thereafter, the green coconuts were stowed in the forward most side of the Torpedo Room since this area had substantial free space without hindering operation of any machinery or crew mobility. That was that, and we forgot all about these nectar-filled South Indian nuts, which had properties to cure anything from blood pressure to even cancer, as some people believe.

The return passage after the refreshing layoff was pretty engaging again, with rarely an 'off day' at sea. We were a very well-trained and cohesive crew with a firm and likeable Captain, and all our tasks were done efficiently and near perfectly. It was with much cheer that we raised[1] the first lighthouse off Bombay, as we returned to our mother port.

Lo and behold, as soon as we tied up alongside our familiar jetty in the Naval Dockyard, then I could espy Commodore S waiting with expectation writ large on his face. Soon enough, his steward came on-board and was directed to collect the 'goodies bag' from the forward compartment. As he left the boat's gangway, I realised the sack was seeming much emptier,

1. The first instance of seeing the projected light from a lighthouse.

but I put it down to my error in judgement.

But no, I had not been mistaken! As we gathered from our EXO later (while we had the customary beer glass after the Ship's company had been secured off), most of the coconuts had disappeared en route from Cochin to Bombay, and the ones remaining were not so "tender ". It is by no stretch of the imagination that we all realised that the 'spoils' had been shared by many on board. The adage of 'finders are keepers' had mostly been obeyed!

Although I did not have any, I always made it a point to sip tender coconut water thereafter whenever I happened to be in Kochi. With a mental thanks to Cmde S for helping me in cherishing the nuts' value!

□

AIR ALERT!

We had finished our classroom Basic Submarines training course followed by the ubiquitous Submarine Board—which awarded us with the coveted Dolphin badge on our uniforms. Thereafter, we had been posted on various boats on either coast of the Navy's Commands. I was borne aboard a slightly older Russian-class diesel-electric sub, which was under Refit and due for a battery set to change under the dockyard hands. We followed a fairly regular routine in harbour, with the occasional OOD duties coming my way.

However, I still needed to sail on an operational boat to obtain my Surface and Dived Watch-keeping certificates—the first steps towards getting to be a qualified submariner. After about six months spent in the naval harbour, I was finally sent on a two-week sortie on another of the Navy's quieter and newer-inducted Russian-class boat.

We had an independent programme, scheduled for patrolling in a typical 'box' much away from our Base port. This was, for me, a top-of-the-line experience, wherein supreme stealth and efficient operational regimes were to be maintained while dived deep under the ocean surface. Boy, this is what I had been trained for – life inside a steel 'shark', operating silently far below the waves.

We also had another officer Lt. Cdr S with us—he was sailing along for his mandatory sea stint as part of his PCO course. Soft-spoken and very professional, he was very dynamic on-board, and I ended up clearing up a lot of my doubts regarding submarine operations, from him. We were to also be sub mates later on when I served as a Watch-keeping Officer under his department as EXO.

Around a week into our dived state, and we had settled into our patrol routine. A diesel-electric boat normally tries to snort during dark hours. But this also meant the watch-keeper on the periscope had to be extra vigilant to scrupulously scan the darkened sea horizon and sky for both surface and air contacts, if any. Also, the sub normally has one Search Periscope in use during snorting, but the Captain could order for a second Attack Periscope for his exclusive use.

I was on the search periscope one such night around 11 pm, arm-muscling the stiff revolving mast—essentially dancing with the 'one-eyed lady'. My eyes had long adjusted to the darkness outside on the surface of the sea (we use red light around the space near the periscopes to achieve this superior retinal sensitiveness during dark hours). The attack periscope had been raised too, and the Captain had had an occasional look on top, before settling down in his chair in the control room.

As I silently rotated the scope, I was concurrently adjusting the elevation angles of the periscope lens to also survey the sky (the rival air element is the biggest concern for a snorting sub and in war could damage or even sink the boat using its torpedoes or depth charges).

For me, the panorama outside was clear of any contacts. After about halfway through my trick, I could make out that someone else was manning the attack periscope, and a sneak peek enabled recognition of S, next to me on the second raised scope mast.

Suddenly I heard the imperceptible but clear voice of Lt. Cdr S: "There is an air contact very near ..." I nearly jumped out of my skin—I had seen nothing till now!

Moments later, I was about to ask him as to which direction

and elevation he was looking at to keep my second eye on this dangerous aerial 'bird'.

It was then that I realised that the Captain (a relatively short but very sprightly old man) had sprung from his corner seat and was near excitedly asking S: "Show me...where." We were not in enemy waters, but a dived sub always assumes its stealthy stance, and an air contact was not good news.

S moved aside and our Captain, after readjusting the scope height to his own, put his eyes onto the eyepiece. He took about a minute or so and then softly exclaimed: "No, no, son, it is a classic conjunction of the Moon and Venus."

S had a relook, as did I, at a much higher elevation, marvelling at the Captain's seasoned eyes, perception, knowledge and analysis.

As the night unravelled, a few more stars beckoned from the sky above. As the sub motored on its usual quiet path, I could not help going back to the Moon. Using a far higher magnification, I carefully etched the 'Bunny on us Earthlings' only Moon a far distance away.

S, later on, joked amiably in the compact Wardroom that he had had a long break from periscope watches, to make such a mistake—but I assured him I would always be extra vigilant while dancing the one-eyed lady!

It was also my only sighting of the Earth's only natural satellite, in those fifteen odd days.

I did realise later that S and myself had done 'moonlighting' that watch long years back, down in the dark inky blue ocean depths!

□

HOME RUN!

We were selected for our Specialisation course in Anti-Submarine Warfare. I was already a Submariner and I keenly anticipated that this Specialisation Course would further aid me in my Naval future to understand the undersea world. It was to be a year-long program at a scenic South Indian port and Naval Base. We were housed at the nearby Naval Mess and dined at the attached Wardroom Dining Hall.

Life was pretty routine with classroom instructions on five days from morning till lunch; Saturdays generally had us sitting for various assessment tests scheduled after respective subjects. We also occasionally had some practical training scheduled in the afternoon and early evening hours after lunch. Since we were an eclectic mix of Surface Navy, Submariners and Aviator Observers, we could also exchange a lot of notes as regards our previous operational experiences. A lot of us kept in touch long after we had passed out of this Training School.

Different instructors taught us the various nuances of diverse topics such as underwater sound propagation principles, basic Sonar theory and specifications and exploitation of a broad range of sensors and underwater weapons fitted on different classes of Naval ships. Since each had an Exam to be cleared at the end, we did not have much scope to slacken off. However, since very little additional duties came our way, we had a good amount of time to consolidate our newfound knowledge, and of course prepare for the assessment tests.

Lt. Cdr J (I had served alongside him on a Capital Ship as a Midshipman about six years back) was our Instructor for a class

of HELO-launched torpedoes. Since he had had had a pretty good amount of experience of handling, preparing and loading of this type of 'fish', his classes were quite profound.

One fine afternoon, he was telling us about the various modes for the Homing Head[1] of this particular torpedo. He started with explaining the basic difference between passive and active modes, and then went on to how the weapon changed modes during various phases of its attack as it initially registered the underwater target 'Contact', then went into a 'Detect' mode and thereafter pursued a fleeing target till the final hit.

It was a balmy day (the port lies near to the Equator so has more than its share of warm and humid weather), and the drone of the overhead fans further accentuated the sense of somnambulistic fervour pervading through our classroom. To give credit, some of us were trying hard to focus on the import of the Instructor's words, however with not much degree of success.

"Lt G, please stand and position yourself right across me in a straight line", suddenly came the Instructor's slightly louder voice. This was me and I (roused from a near half-asleep state) scrambled up and did as directed.

Lt. Cdr J was around 5 metres from me, and he with a 'Watch how the torpedo behaves", started slowly approaching me head-on. Meanwhile, he intoned "Ting Tak, Ting Tak, Ting Tak," (mimicking the transmissions of the Homing Head) as he came nearer. Around 2 metres away and he suddenly started at a much more rapid pace 'Ting Tak, Ting Tak, Ting tak..." like a metronome, concurrently gesticulating with his hands... Within seconds he had nearly collided with me! The 'fish' had found its mark and a 'target' destroyed!

That day is still fresh on my mind because of a Naval style Home Run...!

☐

1. The head section has the sonar, for locating, tracking and homing onto a target.

RIFLING THROUGH!

The specialisation course for training in Anti-submarine Warfare had started for our batch of 16-odd officers. Located at a major South Indian scenic port, the Training School had brought us all back at the place where we had trained on-board the Cadet Training Ship about six years ago. Unlike a Naval Ship's on-board schedule, the routine here at the Training School was far easier with focus on classroom instructions and successful completion of various Assessment Tests to obtain the Certificate of completion after the year-long programme. We also could use our holidays to bike and hike around the picturesque roads along the Western Ghats.

Now, there was an important milestone in our training programme which involved a tough competition between various training schools including ours, Navigation and Direction, Communication, etc., all located at the Naval Base. The hallmark of this contest was the drill performance to be executed by the under-trainee officer group of respective schools.

The drill rehearsals were generally conducted either in the early morning or in the afternoon sessions. Most of us all were rusty in drill manoeuvres (the previous intensive drill and parades practice had been during our cadets' and, to some extent Mids' times about five-six years back). So much so that the drill parade instructors had their hands full to get us all up to the mark. Step synchronisation, cutlass drill, and rifle drills were all rehearsed to achieve as perfect movements as possible.

Our class included an officer Lt. Bhatt—a very bright, earnest and intelligent Aviator Observer. One fine day, we were all lined up on the Drill Square for a near-final rehearsal of Rifle Drill. The fairly weighty DP 7.62 mm Rifles[1] had to be used to conduct ceremonial salutes for various senior officers, who would be attending and reviewing the parade. It was a pretty humid and uncommonly windless afternoon, and we could feel the sweat trickling down our backs and wetting the inside of our uniforms. However, the enthusiasm was very high and everyone coveted the Best School trophy—so the effort was not lacking.

The Drill Instructor along with an Instructor from our Training School was supervising and coordinating our drill. Essentially our line of officers and the Drill Rifles had to be in perfect synchronicity for all movements whether at rest or while carrying out the step-by-step motions for the salutes. During one such umpteenth (as it seemed then) inspection, the Drill Instructor Senior Sailor suddenly barked out from one end of our line: '*Ek, do, teen...batt peechche*[2]." At this Lt. Bhatt immediately shifted himself a bit back on the line. However, the irate Instructor repeated his order!! Lt. Bhatt repeated his slight backward step—but to no avail.

With a third repetition of his order, the Instructor rapidly came towards Lt. Bhatt and with a practised motion, pushed his rifle butt a bit back. This was also accompanied by a much-irritated look by the instructor, for Bhatt's benefit!!

The case of the mistaken identity had been solved as we finally finished off a good Rifle Drill rehearsal!

□

1. Drill practice rifles, whose firing pins have been removed.
2. Hindi phrase meaning "No. 1,2,3...rifle butts back".

GOA GONE!

I was posted on-board one of the Navy's latest diesel-electric submarines. Being a Weapon's Officer, I had charge of a team of highly professional torpedo and other armament crew, with whom I shared a lifelong bond, even much after I had been transferred to another shore appointment.

Now, I also had the charge of Casing Officer—one which entailed responsibilities of maintenance and upkeep of the casing fittings, especially the sonar transducers and the boat's log. Since the salt-laden waters of the vast ocean depths (in which the sub operated for long stretches) was relentless in its erosive and abrasive power, my department and I had their work cut out. Paint peels, stuck bollards, replacement of frayed ropes, cutting off the occasional fishing net tangled inside the casing—we had everything on our plate. Battle-hardened submariners as I imagined myself to be, even the odd seemingly menial task was our 'part of the ship", and I always had a tremendous sense of accountability to the EXO for ensuring tip-top status.

The Casing Officer's station for entering and leaving harbours was on the forward part of the Casing, overseeing letting-go of ropes during unberthing, and fastening of the four boat's securing hawsers, once alongside a jetty or another vessel. The work was often at some risk especially when the ropes were under considerable tension due to frequent manoeuvring of the submarine when securing or unberthing from a jetty or pier. Rainy weather also added to the slickness

of the bare casing deck (which did not have the guard rails, which prevent overboard incidents on surface ships). Also, night-time harbour entries or departures especially demanded extra vigilance on our part.

One such time and we were berthed at Marmagoa port—that 'Eastern Hawai'i. Having had a very refreshing (Goa always is) three-day break from a two-week-long sea sortie, we were primed to leave harbour during early morning hours. It was still dark, and while the mostly *feni*-laden Goans snored away in their tranquil haven, the casing party gulped the boat's Cook's freshly prepared strong cups of coffee.

We had to prepare ourselves for about two hours to stay on the Forward and Aft Casing, till everything had been stowed and secured away after we unberthed and departed away from the port limits. A slight drizzle had started, and I took mental notes to check each lifebelt of the casing crew. After all, the only thing standing between a man fallen overboard and Davy Jones' Locker was this life-saving belt, some of which had a knack of occasionally not inflating satisfactorily at crucial times.

Following SOPs, the Coxswain announced the order for Casing Party to muster on the sub's casing deck. After all evolutions of preparing the boat for sea[1] were over. I was the first one on the casing top, and along with my Petty Officer In-charge, started checking the crew's lifebelts. Most of the crew were up and running with one odd sailor still rubbing sleep off his eyes (he had avoided the early morn caffeine).

But to our consternation, we realised that one of the casing crew was missing. On checking with the Coxswain, we were informed that the missing member was the Chief Cook, who would bc up in a jiffy after serving the Captain (who was already on the Bridge) a second black coffee.

1. A comprehensive series of checks and inspections to ready the submarine for diving.

Time was ticking, and we went about singling up the sub's ropes and standing by to attend to the ropes upon orders from the Bridge, I was by now quite irritated by the Cook's non-appearance and was contemplating asking the Bridge to send him up pronto.

Soon, however, we were caught aback when we espied the Coxswain himself escorting the Cook onto the casing! And it was evident both had not yet fully recovered from Goa's (oh-that Siren) libations and were having a running feud on an extremely slick and dangerous Forward Casing!

Thanks to the Goan Gods and our small prayers, we were spared any untoward incidents as the sub rocked and rolled (Goan libation?) out into the slow swell of the Arabian Sea, and headed north towards Bombay.

I realised that day what running a 'tight ship" meant!

□

ENOUGH TO GO AROUND!

We were on a significantly long patrol aboard our submarine somewhere in the Arabian Sea. The crew had fallen into the routine of watch-keeping at sea, doing routine maintenance, cleaning the ship, etc. Meal timings were especially welcome, since our cooks were good at their job and one could catch up on 'galley gossip', watch a movie on the DVD player and generally chat around with others.

The Captain—a bearded dark and lean Malayali[1]—had nearly finished his dinner plate when he felt like having some more of the excellent *tandoori* chicken. The other officers had cleared the small Wardroom, and the old man felt a little sheepish in asking for the second. Notwithstanding his reservations, he beckoned to the Wardroom Steward and pointing to the now empty chicken bowl asked: "*Kaafi Hai*?" (This is a Hindi term meaning whether there is enough of the stuff to go around). The steward nodded his head up and down, indicating the affirmative.

"*Leke aao*", (Hindi for a directive to bring on the item) said the Captain. The steward dutifully bowed and went back to the galley to do the needful.

Time passed, the Captain shifted to an old Western classic on the DVD player and became engrossed in Clint Eastwood's *Dirty Harry*, as the submarine cruised at slow speed down at the ocean's deeper depths. Although a patient man, the Captain could not help calling out a bit loudly for the Steward

1. People native to Kerala (state in south India).

from the galley, after about ten minutes.

Steward replied that he was on his way, and with a flourish laid a cup of steaming black coffee in front of the Captain, on the Wardroom dining table!

To say the Captain was flummoxed was an understatement. Anyway, he gulped down the coffee and left without a word, back to his single bunk cabin.

What had transpired was that the Steward, a Haryanvi Jat[1], had taken the Captain's order as the English 'Coffee', and served the same accordingly. It also came through the galley gossip later on that he was, for some reason, uncharacteristically cut up with Captain that day!

The incident was indeed 'Kaafi Hai' for our funny bones during the rest of our sea sortie under a Captain whose occasional humorous utterings were otherwise of the driest kind!

□

1. Ethnic group of people native to south Asia including from India, Balochistan etc. Haryana is a northern Indian state.

DREA-MURMUR!

I was the Weapons and Armament Officer on-board the latest state-of-the-art submarine of the Navy. Our Captain (recently taken over Command) was a quirky veteran, and that could be an understatement.

His behaviour towards subordinate officers was brusque at many times, but he always treated us in a thoroughly professional manner and left the softer HR aspects to the highly competent and affable EXO. Captain had also served on this same class of boats as a Commissioning crew Navigator and was fully aware of the platform's capabilities and maneuverability.

Now, the Captain's Standing Orders laid down the events at sea for which he had to be informed immediately. To aid this, his small individual cabin (his cabin was the only private personal space on the sub) was situated just about three feet from the OOW's post. Also, his cabin had a communication module (connected to the main intercom system) enabling two-way reception and transmission of sound. Normally, we would use this channel to inform and make reports to him, whenever relevant, as per orders.

Once, we were at sea for a longish patrol and had settled down into our dived watch routine. Silently cruising like a shark in her element, the two-year-old operational sub was like any other watery denizen so far as the vast ocean was concerned. She was our Mother; all of us nestled in her womb, going about our professional duties in a clockwork fashion. The depths added stability vis-a-vis roll and pitch. Additionally, the relatively slow speeds of the boat transformed our small world into an air-conditioned cocoon chock-a-block with equipment and machinery, while flowing along in Lord Varuna's domain.

I was on the middle watch and was closed up at the Control Room. My area of activity included adjusting of the steering and depth control, as also monitoring done for any alarms for hydraulics, engineering or electrical malfunctioning of the sub's myriad and complex systems. I also had to regularly update our position on the chart and listen out for any contact reports by the sonar watch-keeper.

It was getting to be a pretty dull watch, and I was about to send for a cup of coffee (the middle watch is generally the most sleep-prone trick) when the hitherto silent sonar post came alive. And since the reported contact was classified as a likely warship, it was an occasion to report to Captain ASAP.

I immediately wordlessly rehearsed the full information for the report, and within seconds, repeated it over the mike on the intercom system. Normally, the Captain would give his acknowledgment pretty quickly, and I went back to have a further look at the sonar display to monitor the track of the contact.

However, a full minute passed, and no "Roger[1]" response came from the other end. Now, I had to take the next step—leave my chair in the Control Room, and physically deliver the report to the Captain. Calculating my absence from my post at about just 15 odd seconds, I went up to the Captain's cabin door and after a soft knock, opened it a bit.

It was dark inside, and I could espy the Captain fast asleep on his bunk bed. Anyway, I quickly reported the information pretty loudly, as I assessed. The Captain shuffled a bit, and then to my mild surprise, suddenly sat up bolt-upright with the blanket fully over his head like a shrouded hoodie.

1. A standard form of acknowledgement on Naval units akin to 'Ok, got it'.

"Toh kya hua[1]?" Came his murmured response!! Further nonplussed, I repeated my report, and finally after about fifteen seconds, his soft "Roger" actually enabled my sigh of relief.

Later on, the EXO (who also had served alongside the Captain on a similar boat nearly a decade back) mentioned that it could have been a case of the subconscious hazing between a dream world and reality. Further experiences with the same Captain at sea (recounted in the next few anecdotes) provided significant proof to validate this theory.

I mentally did categorise the 'Old Man' as a Drea-murmurer, after that!

□

1. Hindi phrase meaning, "So what happened?"

FIRE ALARM!

Submariners by nature are an informal lot regarding the uniform for the day. On our daily on-board routine, we were habituated to wearing black shoes with non-skid soles. To us, it all made sense so far as physical safety was concerned whilst traversing and working in the cramped conditions inside the boat. The engineering personnel found the shoes a godsend for long hours of work in the labyrinthine, greasy and oil-slicked deck of the machinery room. Moreover, overalls and even the disposables (normally worn only when at sea) were fair game especially during the monsoon season of Mumbai. They formed a far drier and comfortable alternative to our soaked white uniforms, which we normally wore while travelling from place of residence to the berthed submarine inside the dockyard.

Now, a new Commander-in-Chief was in the saddle and he had some unique requirements of his own. One day in the week was reserved as No. 8s[1] to be worn by all Naval personnel during working hours. And, horrors, the shoes had to be pristine white canvas shoes as per Navy Regulations.

The diktat was discussed in-house amongst many grumblings, the chief tirade being that the Navy normally always allowed a flexible rig as per on-board and work requirements. Anyway, we got back to dusting off and cleaning up our pair of white shoes (hitherto rarely used except on

1. A regulation Navy uniform involving white half shirts and shorts along with white knee-length stockings and white shoes.

ceremonial occasions). Since each of us had a small on-board personal locker to us, stowing the maintained shoes wrapped in cellophane and polythene was not much of a hitch.

Our Captain, who was a veteran with nearly 20 years clocked with the Navy, used to traverse by a shared minivan from his residence to the submarine or shore office. He was thus spared the persistent waterlogged streets of monsoonal Mumbai and also the resultant efforts to maintain a clean pair of white shoes on 'those days'.

It thus transpired one rainy 8s working day that our EXO was caught unaware when he received an early morning call from the Captain, who summoned him pronto to his house for an emergency not covered by any Naval SOP[1].

What had happened was that the Captain had woken a bit late that morning, and to top it, he had an early morning call-on on the C-in-C. Desperate and nearly panicky, he had quickly lathered his white shoes with canvas polish fluid. But the hurried job resulted in excess wetness, which now needed to be dried off fast. With excess humidity in the air, he had nearly no choice but to dump the canvas shoes inside his trusted microwave oven. With his characteristic determination to have a quick and effective solution, he put the timer and temperature settings to the maximum and went for his bath.

But he had to rush back out of the shower within less than a minute. His shoes had caught fire inside the oven!

However, things were managed thereafter in the nick of time by the EXO, whose super-efficient logistician organisation produced a shiny white, albeit a bit tight, shoes pair for the Captain.

Thus it was that the EXO saved a rainy day from turning too hot for an otherwise affable and cool Captain!

□

---

1. Standard operating procedure.

SCOPE UP!

I was borne on a medium-sized diesel-electric[1] submarine as a Weapons and ASW Officer. The sub was fully operational and we were away at sea most of the time, with short stays in harbour.

During one such long sea patrol, we were into our twentieth day in dived state, when our Captain directed a stint at periscope depth, to have a look topside on the sea surface. The sea was calm and the boat steered beautifully through the glassy sea.

Now, the Engineering department sailors seldom see the outside world in a dived submarine, busy as they are with watch-keeping and routine maintenance schedules in the Machinery Room. So, it was that the Captain decided to allow these sailors to have a look through the Search Periscope turn by turn, for about a minute or so each. The staff was more than overjoyed, especially after three weeks of relatively monotonous days in the dived sub.

As time wore on, the line of people waiting patiently for their turn at the periscope started thinning; we went off to tend to our respective departmental work, and the Captain immersed himself in long-pending paperwork.

One of our LMEs[2] was at the periscope, slowly turning all

1. Submarines, which run on battery power, with batteries being charged by diesel generators.
2. Leading Mechanic Engineer, which is a junior rank for a sailor of the Engineering department.

around when he suddenly exclaimed that he could see some trees.

The Captain nearly jumped out of his chair-nobody in their wildest dreams could expect such sightings thousands of miles out on the high seas! As the news spread, the Combat Centre became crowded fast.

Navigator, a seasoned and cool guy, took over the Search Periscope from the sailor, and after a quick look, finally enabled a rational explanation. "Sir, the sailor is seeing the Attack Periscope", said he.

What had happened was that the sailor, manning the Search Periscope, had viewed the raised attack periscope, which was located aft of the search scope: And the Attack Periscope mast had been done up recently with a special camouflage paint in a polka-dot pattern, thence the tree-like appearance!

We had a rare occasion of a 'dry oasis' mirage out at Sea!

□

TURTLE AHOY!

I was appointed as the Weapons Officer on one of the Navy's recently commissioned submarines. The officer lot on-board had also mostly all changed recently, and we had a new Old Man in the saddle. However, most of us (bar a few undertraining OJT officers) had served on these classes of boats before, so we were pretty familiar about operating on this potent undersea platform.

Our Captain of the sub had recently finished command of an older Russian-class sub before his appointment on-board our boat. He (reputations follow quickly in the most professional submarining Arm of the Navy) had his quirks but was also business like—demanding the best from us and the sailors crew. We completed our shakedown sailings with him on the chair and soon were sailing off for regular patrols and exercises with our sister ships of the Naval Command's fleet.

One such month-long patrol found us on an independent surveillance patrol in our designated 'box'. The routine was not an unfamiliar one for most of us—a three watch duty roster, and closing up at our duty posts at various times (time was in any case just relative inside the dived boat with only the on-board clock giving us some semblance of day and night) for Action Stations. Soon most of us periscope watch-keepers grew accustomed to heightened awareness at night times, with sometimes sporadic and other times pretty long sleeping stints in the day.

After a mostly 'uneventful' sojourn, we headed back to our base port of Bombay. Two days off the port, the Captain ordered some surfacing time for the sub. Since we were now far nearer our coast, this was not giving anything away[1], and we slowly broke the surface after ascending through the inky sea depths. As the upper lid leading to the bridge was opened, the first waft of a slightly fishy smell and the sea breeze struck our welcoming noses. The impatient smokers made their quick trip to the bridge, after the all-clear and specific orders from the OOW.

It was an excellent bright and pleasant day at sea and the EXO (ever dynamic and empathetic) allowed the crew a much-needed swim and bathe in the sea.

Most of the off-duty personnel jumped into the water next to the bulk of our boat, with a spare hawser cast in the water around acting as a barrier for any stragglers moving out of the safety zone. Some even preferred to jump off from the about five-metre-high sail top into the water below. The Captain had already ordered the motor to be stopped and our boat lay quite motionless—swaying ever so slightly in the very smooth swell of the Arabian Sea.

About half an hour into the mass sea bath and one of our cooks (just fresh out of the sea swim) informed Bridge that something significantly large and black was being carried by the low waves towards the sub's aft. Since the boat's rear had the single motor and the rudder and aft planes[2], which had to be kept clear of any fouling[3] at all times, the Captain on the Bridge trained his binoculars onto the indicated object for a closer look.

"It's a large dead turtle—let us get it on-board", said he.

1. A submarine is especially vulnerable to detection when it is on surface.
2. Every submarine is equipped with a pair of planes at the stern. These are used to aid in diving or surfacing the boat.
3. Any object, rope, or flotsam that can hinder the operation of the planes or propeller.

Some of us on the Bridge exchanged querying looks but also realised presciently that the dead reptile would be added to our sub's crew for the rest of our passage back. The spotter cook (a hefty strong swimmer) enthusiastically got hold of the about metre-long carcass; the equally dedicated sailors on the casing had soon enough hitched a rope onto one of the turtle's flippers and got it hoisted on-board.

We were just wondering as to what to do next (stowing a dead turtle on board, after all, was not covered under any SOP), when I suddenly realised that the Old Man had climbed down the 15-feet-long ladder inbuilt on the sail side, and had made his way forward to have a closer look at this expired sea denizen. We could make out some deep conversation between the Captain and the cook.

Before we could fully grasp as to the next intentions regarding the shelled creature, one of the casing party sailors had taken out a diver's sharp-edged knife, and lopped off the turtle's head! The ensuing gush of blood and gore was a sight to see and took most of us aback.

The Old Man had meanwhile clambered up back on the bridge and apprised us that he planned to get the headless turtle ashore and hand over to the Prince of Wales Museum for taxidermy and display! Stunned we were, to make an understatement.

Anyway, the turtle was secured within the free flooding space inside the forward casing with strong rope lashings and we dived the sub soon after clearing the casing of all other crew.

Came the next day, and we surfaced, being very near and in shallower depths off Bombay. It was then that the putrid odour hit us! As I (who was the officer who opened the Upper Lid during any surfacing) stood on the Bridge and tried to reason with myself as to what could be raising such a stink, the source dawned on me along with the first rays of the rising

Sun. The decapitated turtle had spent a full night underwater in the sub's casing, and Nature's scavenging bacteria had gone to work. The lack of the head and a gaping ripped open hole in the dead animal had made matters far worse. However, there was no escape, and as the Captain joined on the Bridge, it was clear he was not one to rescind his intention of donating to the Museum's curator.

As it happened, we berthed at our jetty inside the naval dockyard, with a far more malodorous addition to our call sign than others were habituated to. The curious shore party staff did ask some of our crew regarding the smell, but not much was divulged.

The dead reptile had meanwhile been unsecured and was being washed when the senior officer present on the shore could not bear it anymore and had a quick talk with the Captain. And, as it many times happened with the best-laid plans of men and mice (and sometimes of dead sea turtles too), the Old Man instructed us to dispose of the carcass as early as possible. The cook was again allotted this task, and with his usual zeal he cut it up into little pieces and threw them into the water. The shell, however, was carted off by a collector from the dockyard and is probably kept as a curio somewhere after methodical preparation and painting.

Yes, people nearly 'turned turtle' on the jetty that day due to the 'legalised' overnight stowaway on our boat!

□

WELL DONE!

Appointed as the Weapons Officer on-board the latest sub of the Navy, I was fully charged up and enthusiastic about my all-important role as one of the specialist officers' crew on board. After all, of what use is a 'steel shark' without its business end–torpedoes and all.

The boat was starting its sailing operational cycle and we were seeing less and less of our base port. Our Captain tried his best to undertake the sea sorties within weekdays, so that the personnel could at least have one day out of a two-day-long weekend, at home with their families. Since I was one of only two officers still boarded and lodged at the Command Officers Mess (we were both bachelors)—we ended up adjusting weekend OOD duties with others in the roster.

Within around two months of my joining the 'ship', the Practice Torpedo Firing season started in the right earnest. And my department was in the thick of it. For me—fresh back from year-long specialisation training—this was manna from heaven. Theory was put into hardcore practice and many a lesson was learned. Most days and quite a few nights were spent at harbour and sea in planning and executing of these 'fish shoots'[1]. Additional work included sending detailed and pretty voluminous reports of these firings, to our shore analysis unit.

On one of such week-long practice firing sorties, we had had a packed schedule of different exercises. This involved

1. Naval slang for the practice torpedo firing exercises.

tracking and carrying out simulated attack runs on fleet ships. Since the primary and biggest weapon of a sub is invisibility and surprise, our crew got into the routine of being closed up at Action Stations at a moment's notice. For all practical purposes, we were operating in a 'wartime' scenario (a sub's offensive potency and stealth does not allow it any luxury of much slack time in peace, and virtually no let-up during actual war).

It was night time and I was the OOW manning the periscope over a three-hour watch 'trick' in the darkened control room. Since a snorting sub faced heightened danger from airborne 'enemy' elements, my visual surveillance on the 'scope was particularly crucial during this graveyard shift from 1 to 4 am. We could not afford any detection by opposing forces and the Old Man had passed explicit night orders for calling him post-haste when in doubt or sight of even any faintly recognised enemy unit.

I carefully rotated the scope, simultaneously softly instructing the nearby seated Sonar Watch-keeper to be extra alert. Needless to say, he regularly reported the 'underwater picture' to me.

Midway through my watch, I felt a slight air draught near my bare ankles (on subs, comfortable disposable shirts and shorts are worn with just rubber-soled sandals shod feet). I guessed that someone had opened the small deck hatch near the periscope well[1] for some maintenance or cleaning work in the bilges area at the bottommost depths inside the boat. Also, I made a mental note to perform my dance with the 'one-eyed lady' far more carefully to avoid the now open hatch with a near 12-feet vertical drop below.

My eyes however, remained glued to the scope eyepiece with my head under a black skirt-like apron covering the optics equipment. This practice had to be followed to preserve

1. A deep columnar space beneath a periscope, which allows its retraction before diving of the boat.

my night vision from getting disturbed by the tiniest of glares or reflected light from the various glowing dials or any LED indicators of other nearby equipment.

A sudden appearance of a faint moving light glimmer far off in the horizon immediately caused me to point the scope directly towards this 'contact'[1]. I adjusted my optical elevation for better scrutiny and warned the sonar operator and ESM watch-keepers to keep a sharper lookout on this bearing.

A minute passed, and the light spotted on the scope seemed to fade off in the distance with no activity on sonar or ESM. I started relaxing a bit and reset the elevation to a higher level to carry out the standard air sweep[2].

But, even as my tighter hold on the Scope's Rotation Handles[3] loosened a bit, I could feel my feet giving way and started tumbling straight down, as if in slow motion!!

The open well-hatch had done its 'trick' even as mine was ending. I had slid down its maw with my face nearly at deck-level when quick reflexes and fairly fit arm muscles prevented my full free fall and serious injuries including highly possible fractures.

As I gathered myself up, brushing off the slight grease stains on my hands, I realised none of the other watch-keepers had noticed my mishap.

I observed with a sardonic and unconventional nautical twist that:

All's 'Well' That Ends Well!

□

1. Any unit (air, surface or sub surface) detected by a sensor like periscope.
2. A specific sequence of surveillance by the periscope, for an air contact.
3. These are a pair of horizontal handles used for turning the periscope.

IT'S OFFICIAL!

I was posted as the Weapons Officer on a diesel-electric boat at Bombay. I had also recently gotten married and was well into completing nearly a decade in the Navy. We had managed to move into one of the newer married accommodation flats. The flat was spanking new (we were its first inhabitants), but was quite far from the Naval Dockyard, where our sub was berthed. A daily to and fro shuttle bus and the very punctual local train services enabled the transit from home to my unit.

Sailings galore were de-rigor for us since the boat was fully operational. Whatever off time I had was spent in catching up on myriad movies and plays at the famous Prithvi Theatre, along with my wife. We also met up with other of my coursemates who were mostly borne on sea billets at the same base port.

By and by, I was allotted a quarter at the wonderfully located NOFRA (Naval Officers Residential Accommodation). Our 11th floor flat gave a fantastic view of the Arabian Sea, whose shoreline enmeshed with the concretised boundary of the nearby Command Mess. As I got promoted to my next rank, we shifted to a larger fourth floor-located flat within NOFRA itself. It was here that our son was born, and where we subsequently spent around two more years before my transfer to NHQ.

It was only much later after our marriage that one fine day my wife suddenly confided: "I always thought that Naval officers work out of offices while only the sailor staff sail...!"

I was slightly miffed and flummoxed, to say the least, and proceeded on a short explanation about our operational organisation.

Now she well knows that both officers and sailors are in the 'same boat' when at sea.

□

JETTING AROUND!

I was having a hiatus in an otherwise long operational seaborne appointment tenure. Posted at the Submarine Squadron HQ Base at a large Naval Command, life, however, was not dull. Daily plannings and briefings for practice torpedo firings of various submarines of the squadron took up the major part of my working hours.

As time flew, the mild winter season gave a welcome relief from the hot humid weather and then the incessant rainy monsoons of Bombay. This meant calmer seas for the fleet units and easier recoveries of the practice 'fish'. We from the HQ and Base staff also found life cooler and comfortable. During one such January day, the Cdr (SM)[1] instructed me to ensure the tip-top operational availability of the Submarine Motion Control Simulator[2]. This Simulator was to be the piece-de-resistance for the visiting NDC[3] trainee officers in a week.

Now, the Simulator (accessed through a flight of metal stairs) was a set-up having two partially separated compartments. While one was the Combat Centre of the simulated class of boats, the other mimicked the Control Room.

Came the day, and after the introductions and mutual

1. A Commander-ranked officer responsible for all operations of submarines of the Squadron.
2. This refers to a mock-up functioning simulator for Control Room of the submarine.
3. National Defence College—this is the nodal and premier training institution for senior officers.

pleasantries, it was the turn of my 'part of ship' The group of 10 visiting officers was nearly split halfway—each to be accommodated between the two compartments inside the Simulator rig.

As soon as the OI/C—a young Lieutenant (sitting at his controls in a Porta-cabin outside the huge Simulator rig)—fed the settings for starting and operating it, we were on our way inside the Simulator. Sea states were varied to have a feel of choppier monsoon waters off Mumbai, and turn by turn, each of the senior trainee officers had a go at planing and steering[1] the 'boat'.

Since the trainee mix was tri-service, the curious queries (even from salt-experienced grizzled Naval Commodores) asked of me, were equally diverse. I had prepared well, as had the sailor staff who manned the various sensor and machinery posts inside, so it was a cinch for us.

An IAF fighter pilot settled down into the seat meant for the Aft Planes and Steering Rudder control. I noticed he was in a flight suit overall and had an ugly scar on the back of his neck and shoulders. Immediately empathetic (he probably had had a previous bad aircraft accident or even a flame-out crash), I took the foreplanes' control seat and started explaining the various sensor repeaters in front of us, as well as the basic process of taking the sub up or down inside the ocean depths. I also observed that he was most enthusiastic and vibrant about starting the manoeuvres. Finally, I also explained that the loss of depth would be gradual, with depths being called off and reported by me at each 10 metres interval.

The OI/C informed me that sea state had been set at a significantly high level, and speed at around 10 knots, which was pretty high for the otherwise slow-moving 'boat'. Even as I shared that we would be planing from a depth of 100 to

1. Refers to use of planes to dive or surface the boat and course changes as required (steering).

40 metres, I could espie my side seat controller put the lock buttons on his bullhorn to 'off' position[1].

And then, it happened! Aft planes were instantly put to max up angle, and steering fully to starboard. The whole rig launched into an upward angle of 30 degrees (and increasing), and I could hear somebody's notebook falling off the chart table in the Combat Centre. Within seconds, the sub was on 'Surface'!

As the session ended, the fighter pilot gave me a warm handshake.

One of a lifetime dream occasion to experience a fighter jet dogfight tactic under the sea—I had finally got that too!

□

1. Refers to the control system (for planning and steering), shaped like a pair of bull horns. These have small buttons to lock or unlock them for use.

AS THE CROW FLIES!

The very prestigious and 'happening' International Fleet Review (IFR) was slated to be held at Bombay (now Mumbai). Around 20 odd nations from nearly all the continents, had accepted the invitation sent by our Navy.

We were to play host across nearly a week, to around 30-odd foreign warships, along with the top brass of the Naval and other military forces from these nations. The task was an onerous and challenging one, even for the well-oiled administrative, logistical and technical might of the Navy. In fact, in the inaugural meeting to discuss the POA, the C-in-C made it amply clear that there was very little scope for any errors, and all other works on ships and shore units were to be secondary to those for the upcoming IFR.

Various events on the IFR itinerary had been delegated to different units. Our sub (I was the EXO) had been earmarked to prepare for the first inaugural reception—a tea party to be hosted by the Governor of Maharashtra. And the main hallmark at this party were group photographs of visiting ships' Captains and another of all the top brass of our and guest Navies.

Our boat was under Dockyard hands for a Long Refit. A number of our sailors had been allotted other extraneous duties of jetty security and a few also on temporary transfer to other operational subs. I had my work cut out. However, an extremely efficient Coxswain and his team of other ratings instilled the confidence in me for meeting all IFR work deadlines.

Now, each of the group photographs was to have a backdrop with all attendee nations' flags fluttering high above the human subjects. Our chief and most important priority was to thus get a wooden flag stand manufactured, along with a requisite number of poles and flags of each attendee nation. This seemed easy on paper. However, as we progressed, it dawned that an already overstretched dockyard would need to be coordinated and closely liasoned with, to enable installation of this two-photograph worth flag stand on the event day at the Raj Bhawan lawns.

As it transpired, lots of tense moments arose, and both push and pull (or is it warp and weft) were used, to get things ship-shape with regards to the 'flag stand' in a time-bound manner. It was with a significant sense of accomplishment that we finally laid out the wooden stand, and the flag-bearing poles, on our sub's berthing jetty, for our Captain's final nod.

We 'sailed through' his critical eyes, and I gave a befitting BZ[1] to our team of hard-working, resourceful and diligent sailors.

Came the inaugural event in the IFR calendar—the Raj Bhawan Tea Party. I oversaw the rigging of the flag stand for a completion, and then we were off to the Governor's residence. The full paraphernalia for the flag stand accompanied us, on-board a military truck.

It was my first personal visit to the Raj Bhawan, and I was awestruck. The vast vista of the lawns adjoined by the Arabian Sea face will remain etched in my memory as one of the most scenic locales ever. Even as I was marvelling, our ever quick sailors' team rapidly set up the stand base, fitted all the flag poles in their respective sockets, and placed the entire flag stand right behind the seating arrangement earmarked for the group photographs. And then it was time for a quick lunch (packed meals had been brought along for the purpose) at a

1 ∫-Bravo Zulu indicating 'Well done'.

shady place under a tree adjoining the lawns. We were nearly there—the final step just involved handing over the set-up to the Raj Bhawan officials, nearer to the party timing, which was still a couple of hours away.

But as the saying goes: "Best-laid plans of men and mice...", trouble of an aerial sort was winging its way across. Even as I was contemplating a small post-lunch nap (military personnel learn fastest how to catch up on sleep even in near-death situations), I espied something that could have made me give stiff competition to any jack-in-the-box.

A crow (hopefully not a Raj Bhawan pet), had perched itself precariously on one of the flag pole top. It was also continuously inspecting the uppermost edge of the flag where it was rigged up onto the pole. A fairly strong sea breeze (otherwise a blessing for cooling off from the balmy humid Bombay weather) added to the forces acting on the particular pole. Ergo, the flag pole was about to topple down, probably onto adjoining poles. Horrors! One or more poles could even break in the process! We had a few extra poles, but they could be of shorter length or of worse finish. I cursed Murphy, crow, and wind God, in that order.

The ever sprightly Coxswain, as was his wont, sprang lithely, and caught and steadied the teetering flag pole in the nick of time. The crow tried to hold onto its perch, decided the nearby trees were probably shadier and flew off.

As we shouted our 'Bravo' for the Coxswain, and I observed the welcome sight of the first of the Governor's staff ambling across towards us, I thought out aloud-

'This was not a day for the Crow's Nest!'

□

TRADE SECRET!

The Commander-in-Chief staff informed our Captain about the impending 2 days sea sortie by the Admiral onboard our sub. The boat was fully operational and all specialist Executive branch officers had served with the 'Old Man' who also had a previous Executive Officer tenure onboard the same submarine. Just some sprucing up of internal spaces, paintwork on the outer hull and casing, instructions to Ship's Company - and we were ready to go.

The C-in-C boarded on the due day, ushered in with the customary naval piping. He was led inboard-entry through the open Upper Lid, via the 5 metres of vertical metal ladder down into the CIC and thereon to the small but utilitarian single bunk Captain's Cabin (only the 'Old Man' has the total privacy of a room to himself onboard the boat). Captain had shifted to the 2 bunked port Exo's Cabin, with the rest of us 5 officers in the starboard Cabin.

The schedule of refreshments, lunch, evening tea and dinner for the first day and night, had been chalked up to a T, by ever efficient Exo. As the Admiral changed into the ever comfortable submarine disposables, the Chief Cook and Steward were working like clockwork inside the congested galley. The Captain's special crockery and cutlery had been shined for the occasion, including the silver salvers and spoons.

It was around 11 am now, and the Navigator was busy in the CIC, charting out courses for the all important upcoming practice torpedo firing serial for the next day. The 'Old Man' and Exo were also around, gearing up for the Admiral's walk around in all compartments from forward to aft. Soon, the C-in-C quietly joined the submarine officers, walking the few feet from Captain's Cabin to CIC in sandal shod feet.

This was the Steward's cue. Within minutes, he served up drinks and snacks, balancing the glassware and crockery on a round silver tray. Each tall glass had a bubbly and clear frothy liquid chilled to the right temperature. The Admiral (must have been pretty thirsty since we had been at sea for well over 3 hours in the humid sticky heat of Mumbai) picked up his napkin wrapped glass, finished off the refresher at one go, and requested for a refill. Steward G Singh, past master at VIP visits, quickly did so, and the second glass was emptied at a slower pace. The snacks were consumed with equal alacrity. The walk around was conducted next, and went off quite well.

C-in-C returned to CIC, and asked for Steward G Singh. Apron-clad G. Singh, who was now laying the tiny Wardroom table for the sumptuous lunch spread, arrived after a minute to the CIC. Upon seeing him, Admiral- with a broad smile and twinkle in his eyes, asked him "G Singh, what is the magic recipe for this superb drink?" Pat came the Steward's reply—*"Sir, woh mein aapko baad mein bataoonga."*[1]

I immediately focused on the Admiral's reaction and looked at the Captain out of the corner of my eye. While the former was already on his way back to Captain's Cabin for much needed rest before lunch, the Old Man had a slightly raised eyebrow.

The C-in-C visit was a huge success, especially made so by a precise torpedo firing exercise on Day 2.

Zingo—that was the name of the popular drink served in the CIC that day (and on many later occasions).

G Singh's reply had been an equal Zinger–a secret more closely guarded than the Charge Books held onboard!

□

1. Translated from Hindi it means – "I will tell you later"

Section-5

MONKEYING AROUND!

I had just been appointed on the Staff of an important procurement Directorate in our Naval Headquarters. This was a vastly different kettle of fish from the operational life on-board submarines, of which I had had experience over the past decade. Here, one had to understand that the Naval part was just one cog in the whole wheel of the Defence Ministry. Files (which nearly multiplied at times like flies!) needed to be constantly completed and pushed out to the next addressee, at various speeds. And sometimes keeping track of the movement of these files across different Naval hierarchies and layers of bureaucracy was more challenging than keeping tag with enemy targets whilst underwater on our boats!

Anyway, I settled in and started as an associate with another slightly senior officer Cdr K (who was also my friend, philosopher and guide throughout my stay at the Directorate). Since he was a totally dedicated and an extremely professional, hardworking officer, I did my best to keep up with his perfectionist orientation for task completion.

Meanwhile, I also gathered that the particular floor, on which we were situated, was particularly welcoming for a group of marauding monkeys. So much so that a visiting very senior officer was heard remarking that the building housed 'both kinds of monkeys'.

Now, one fine evening, Cdr K and I were winding up in the Directorate office (both had returned after umpteen rounds of the Defence Ministry's offices for pushing and clearing various files in preparation for a high-level meeting with foreign OEMs the coming week). It was nearing 7 pm, and as I started switching off fans and lights in the office rooms (the last person to leave had to ensure this routine), Cdr K bid me a brief bye and hurried off out of the office, softly saying he needed to attend a social calling that night. As he quickly walked off along the adjoining corridor, I collected the main door lock and keys (hung inside a small glass-faced cupboard) and began locking the double set of outer main doors.

As I turned towards the exit corridor after the door locking, I saw Cdr K coming back at top gear, one hand gripping his briefcase, and he sported a fairly agitated look. As he came closer, he quickly asked me to open the main doors. Even as I reopened the locks, I could hear him muttering: "Bloody monkeys!"

To my mild surprise, K (reminding me of the same-named Agent in *Men in Black*[1]) lunged behind the door, fished out a long wooden stick and asked me to accompany him through the exit corridor. I re-locked the doors and quickened my steps to keep pace with him (he was a 6-foot-4-inch giant).

As we walked (trotted would have been more apt), he narrated briefly that he had been waylaid by the 'Monkey Group" (a-la King Louis and his followers in *The Jungle Book*[2]) as he had rounded the corner after traversing the exit corridor. The simians had surrounded him and he had taken the only action open under the circumstances—using his swinging briefcase arm as a weapon, and thus giving him the time and opening to revert to the office.

The 'Monkey Stick' (later I was explained that this was the only 'arms' specifically kept in the office for repulsing the rhesus monkeys) was however unused that evening– the red-

1. A popular Hollywood movie series starring Will Smith.
2. The classic book by Rudyard Kipling, now also made into a popular movie.

faced interlopers had vanished from the scene. Our passage out of the building was thereafter uneventful.

The 'Arm and The Man' was the saviour for Cdr K that day—long live GB Shaw!

□

OH, RATS!

I had recently joined on the staff at one of the Submarine Directorates at the Naval Headquarters. This was the hub of all procurement negotiations for past, present and, of course, the future of the Navy's elite Submarine branch. However, the state of the floor and the building we were housed in (a wing of the 'Bhawan' primarily meant for the far bigger Army) left a lot to be desired. Pretty old construction, along with the dubious distinctions of being the 'Monkey Headquarters' a-la the *Jungle Book*, gave a rather decrepit look to our office rooms otherwise choc-a-bloc with important work content. We had to be satisfied with rattling room ACs and oldest model heating units, with care to avoid the overhanging wiring (damaged more due to our simian 'cousins').

It was then that one fine day came the financial sanction for sprucing up our surroundings and office spaces. A quick afternoon beer was shared with the Boss, and strategies carved out for managing the plethora of work to be carried out on our office area in the coming months. It was winter and made things a bit easier since the much-valued individual room ACs would not require to be transported and shifted around during the changing workspace occupation by most officers due to the renovation.

I moved around quite a bit between two rooms since I needed to be around a large glass and metal cupboard drawer filled with most of the important documents of the Directorate. Since my immediate previous long stint on a sea-going submarine also involved staying and operating within cramped spaces and periodic shifts to different cabins, this was grist for the mill.

However, as it turned out, I was not to be third time lucky.

Well halfway into the renovation and repair work, I elected to operate in a separate independent room with its individual AC and was quite surprised that even our senior lot had not vied for it, given its privacy. The reason hit me as I stepped into the room one fine Monday.

An obnoxious stench consisting mainly of a dead rodent's odour assailed me as I closed the door behind me. As I immediately reacted to this nauseous stink with a handkerchief to my nose, my mind's objective side guided me to look for the source of the smell. I called a few Directorate sailors for back-up, and we went to work scouring the room inch by inch. After all, I had to stay and operate from this 'private cabin', (normally only the Captain of a small ship or submarine has a cabin all to himself for herself) for at least two months.

But to no avail—the rodent (most probable culprit could have been a mouse or a rat) refused to be found. We finally also concluded that it could have been buried within the walls of the room (which had also recently been repaired and whitewashed).

Anyway, I called for a big can of room freshener and after a liberal spray, the stench settled down.

I realised the privacy of my office space in the coming days as I was visited only by a very few of my fellow staff who only met when urgently required. And I found myself more amenable to going off on trips to other MoD offices[1] for file 'pushing' (a job hitherto not much liked by me as also by everyone else)!! Also, I started carrying around the faint 'dead ratty' aroma on my clothes!!

1. Ministry of Defence.

Later on, I ruminated that even humans had probably met the same fate—the legend(?) of Emperor Akbar burying alive his son's paramour came to my imaginative mind.

There could not but have been a starker contrast—while Anarkali*[1] *has gained fame due to the lovely dresses named after her, the 'rat'(?)' had only succeeded in enabling a malodorous scent on my dresses!

□

1. The paramour of Jahangir (Akbar's son) who, legend has it, was entombed alive.

SCAT...CAT!

I had recently taken up my appointment as Staff with an important procurement Directorate in Naval HQ. After a wait of around three weeks, we (a two-year-old son apart from his nanny and us couple) got an old but very centrally and well-located government quarters, as our abode. A nearby allotted garage space with lockable doors enabled parking of our family car and oodles of packaging material from our newly unpacked household stuff.

The house on the ground floor had a medium-sized lawn area opposite the main front door. This area was common greens for children of various sizes and ages to play around in the evenings and have an odd game of cricket on cooler weekends.

But it was the private lawn and vegetable garden space at the backyard of the house, which was the ultimate prize. Coming as we were from the multi-storeyed buildings of Mumbai (my previous base), this patch of green area, circumscribed by a neat fencing and a small wicket gate, brightened up even our dourest hot summer evenings and coldest winter afternoons. The gardener was thus instructed to tend to a host of flowers of various bright hues and also help us grow a select few veggies. This, the efficient Mr. Green Thumbs did, and by and by we had most of our daily intake of brinjal, spinach, broccoli and ladies fingers from this patch of earth in the central area of the backyard.

Now, with such luscious crops and colourful flowers,

came the expected litany of pests, rodents and other fauna. Squirrels from a fairly large tree (this grew just inside the perimeter fencing) twittered and made merry in both arboreal and ground modes. Good-sized bandicoots and smaller rats became an eyesore for the gardener since they were voracious eaters and chewers of roots and shoots from the carefully tended vegetable patch.

Mother Nature started working its enormous evolution-honed creative sense. About three months into our stay, a pair of mongooses took up residence along one side of the garden near to the fencing, to complete the ecosystem pyramid. A litter of three to four pups followed. And lo and behold, they started frequenting our toilet-cum-bathrooms through their open backdoors (these needed to be left open after toilet or bath use, since there were no inbuilt exhaust fans for ventilation). These furry and sleek mammals' visits were more frequent during hot summers, as the agile animals relished the coolness of wet bathroom floors.

Life was quite good, my son was growing up right alongside a full mini biosphere of various songbirds, rodents, and the apex predator-mongoose. To add to the menagerie, a pussycat (who had initially given birth to three kittens in our secure garage) shifted house with her young family, to our backyard.

Now, this single mother cat was bringing up her progeny as best as possible with our back garden yard providing both shelter and security. I, a keen observer of animal life, especially felt very elated as we watched both the cat and mongoose families' antics. A plethora of young pups and kittens added a lot of excitement and energetic vibrancy to this evening hub of our backyard.

These were early days—so both the mother cat and the adult mongoose pair (otherwise apex predators in their own rights) were trying to get along as best as possible. For us, of course it was a double boon. Both *Felis catus* and *Herpestes edwardsi* were excellent rodent hunters. They finished off the bigger bandicoots (which eased our ever-vigilant gardener's brows) and the occasional slower squirrel (which put me off as I had a soft corner for these agile and compact tree huggers).

The garden tree had its own share of birdlife ranging from the early morning babblers to the ever opportunistic crows looking to swoop down on any bit of offal or other organic waste from the kitchen, and also clean up remnants of any partially eaten rat. This tree also had a fairly large oval hole on its trunk, about six feet from the ground. We also used to frequently hear the hoots of an owl during late evenings as well as in the dead of night. Naturally, I surmised that the owl was the resident of the tree hole during daytime.

The kittens had grown up and were no longer suckling; they were now trying to hunt down prey on their own but were far clumsier than their expert hunter, mommy cat. She, on the other hand, had lost weight during the long summer months. Now, that autumn was heralding the arrival of the quite cold winter, she was fully into hunting and food gathering. We used to feed her milk in the afternoons and the odd fish fry from our kitchen was also shared on weekends. But she still seemed in a perpetual hungry mode.

One cool afternoon, I was relaxing with a beer glass in the backyard and catching up on my reading. The mongooses were warily poking out their noses from their burrows, watching out for mom cat. I could espie her from the corner of my eyes, ambling around in the veggie patch, probably digging up and chewing on precious vitamin-rich greenery.

Suddenly, I observed her focussed gaze on the tree hole. My senses alert, I put down the morning newspaper and in turn, followed the cat's movements and track. With a few bounds, she started clambering on the angled slant of the tree trunk. An expert climber, she was soon trying to peer down the tree hole.

Wondering what would happen next (I expected the owl to be roosting in its tree hole nest during the day), I waited with bated breath.

And then all hell broke loose!

A small, flashing arrow-like figure hurtled down on mom cat like a bolt from the blue! I realised my mistake then—the tree hole was Woody the woodpecker's property! The bird's stiletto-like beak found a vacant spot on the cat's head between the ears and went to work like a drill.

Mom cat, too stunned by this aerial assault, came sliding down tail-first. Uncharacteristic of her usually sleek and agile movements, her ground landing was quite rough, but she gathered her wits and dashed back towards her kittens, huddled under a ledge jutting out from our house wall at the opposite end of the backyard.

Even as we tended to her bruised head with drying antibiotic powder, I could not help but noting why Sir Reginald Bacon (the pioneer of Naval Aviation) laid stress on and started the first use of aerial elements for the Royal Navy around a century ago.

After all, the small bird had felled the cat-o-nine-lives!

□

SOUR GRAPES!

I was posted on the staff of a shore-based Maritime Training establishment at one of the Navy's main Commands. Being an ASW specialist in the Submarine branch, my expertise was sought on most matters of an 'underwater' nature.

Life was pretty routine, going by the otherwise challenging and tough work schedule of the Navy, especially on sea billets. Boarded and lodged at the nearby Command Officers' Mess (my family was staying put in the quarters at my previous base station), I tried to catch up on my reading, and also forayed across the main city during off days. Long weekend walks up the nearby hilly terrain, afforded an excellent and picturesque view of the port city's harbour entrance. This was a bonus that one otherwise could not enjoy whilst traversing within the harbour channel on a warship or submarine.

Now, the Navy had a policy that all personnel needed to mandatorily undertake small arms practice firings at the shooting ranges of each respective Command. So it was that I was nominated for one such event. The whole evolution also involved transporting various accessory equipment such as the targets, safety helmets, jute cloth, etc., on military trucks from the Naval Base to the about 50 km distant range.

Being the senior-most among the 'firing party', I was graciously offered a seat next to the sailor MTD[1] and the Assistant Command Gunnery Officer, in the cabin of the truck. However, there was a small issue—I had not brought along

1. Military Transport Driver.

my 'Blues Sea Rig' (worn at such practice shoots) from my old base station. Nevertheless, the Navy's other Blues (worn on each Friday at shore establishments to be one with the personnel at sea) came to the rescue. The half sleeves of this rig (as compared to buttoned-down full sleeves of the Sea Rig) were the only minor difference, which was, under the circumstances, a trifle, and passed muster for the day's event schedule. This small variation was, however, to play its part in the unfolding latter moments of the day at the Range.

The shooting range had various configurations laid out for diverse small arms such as pistols, 9mm carbines (scourge of the enemy in real close-quarter battles), automatic SLRs (self-loading rifles) and even the heavy-duty Machine Guns. Since a whole lot of nominated personnel from the entire Command (including those from ships, submarines and air station) had turned up, the Master Chief GI and his Gunnery rates had their work cut out. After all, the calculated quota of bullets had to be expended and empties[∫] collected without any accident or personal injury.

MCGI D was a large built veteran of the Navy, with a booming voice to match, as is wont for most GIs. His strident orders cut across the rat-tat of fired shot volleys and the clamour of a large gathering of blue-shirted Naval officers and sailors.

An introductory instruction session on weapon handling, safeties involved and post-firing drill being done with, it was my turn at the trigger. Three kinds of arms were ready—9 mm pistol (hardest to hit the target with), 9 mm carbine and the 7.62 mm SLR. My gamut also included three types of firing body positions-'standing', 'sitting' (with one knee bent) and the 'lying down. The last required cradling the SLR on two hands with both elbows on the rough ground taking the weight of the rifle. Here, the half sleeved shirt caused me quite some scrapes and bruises in the hot sun, but then what is a battle without injuries.

Now, each series of shoots involved the firing of the weapon, emptying of the gun chamber, and then rushing to the respective targets some distance away to collect the paper 'bullseye' (pockmarked with bullet holes, which one hoped were not due to the neighbouring shooter's stray shots). These brown sheets were assessed for marking of the respective shooter's performance—the targets were, thereafter, repapered over afresh for the next round.

Both my shoots with the pistol and carbine were not very encouraging and some of my fired shots had barely just about clipped the outermost edge of the target. Being an underwater weapons specialist myself (who had conducted such practices for the whole ship's company not so long ago), I was not at all satisfied with this performance. I silently cursed my half sleeved Blues shirt for adding to my discomfiture. The Master Chief GI was, however, surprisingly non-committal regarding the issue, which I put down to regard for my seniority and age.

Determined to be ahead in the 'Learning Curve' I gritted myself for the penultimate SLR shoot, which had a single shot as well as automatic volley firings. I had an innate gut feeling about the MCGI's vast experience across the huge varieties of Naval guns of diverse bores[1]. So it was that as I was taking up the lying prone position, I discreetly inquired from him regarding tips to improve my aim.

'*Sir, angoor ke guchche ki tarah hone chahiye shots iss baar...*"[2] he advised, or, rather ordered in his baritone growl.

With these words ringing in my mind and my assistant ready with an empty helmet next to me to collect ejected empties, I held my breath and let loose my shots at the human tall target erected around 100 yards away. After about seven-eight minutes, which seemed like eons, when the cacophony

1. Naval guns on ships have a diverse range of bores like 30 mm, 6" large guns, etc.
2. Hindi phrase meaning 'Your shots should show up as a bunch of grapes'.

of fired bullets died away and the ALL CLEAR given, we rushed towards our respective target 'Bulls'.

And lo and behold—the marks on my 'Magpie' were clustered together at one side of the brown target paper like a......' bunch of grapes'!

As we retired for the packed lunches under a shady tree nearby, I thanked the MCGI and silently patted myself:

The grapes had not been sour after all!

□

HALT!

I was commanding one of the Navy's latest gas turbine-propelled frigates. These sleek Russian origin warships were equipped with the latest in sensors and firepower. Needless to say, I had a full plate as regards sailing programmes and there was very little spare time otherwise. On the other hand, since the tenure would be probably for a year and a half, I was inwardly thankful for an operational Command tenure (COs majorly dream of mostly seafaring tenures—being the hallmark of one's professionalism in maintaining and running an operational Capital Ship).

Well nearly halftime into my Captain's stint, and we were returning from a week-long sortie. The incessant monsoons had nearly petered out for Mumbai, our Base port. However, as we prepared for entering and final berthing alongside at the Naval harbour, the rain gods decided to welcome us with showers. Like one, every crew member donned their rain suits and closed up at their stations as usual. We, in the Bridge, would be probably spared the wetness, unless one got positioned on the more open Bridge wings. Anyway, I had already got my rain gear stowed near my chair in the bridge, just in case.

As the ship progressed on its near inexorable path towards our usual berth in the Naval Dockyard, the SCO informed me that we had been allotted a different berth from our usual one due to some shifting around of other Naval submarines. This was a common occurrence in the pretty overcrowded tidal basin of the harbour, and I just made a mental note of this information. As the Navigator did slight corrections for our final approach to this new berth, I exchanged the positive part with him—we (the Captain and Navigator share the major responsibility of navigating the ship to an alongside berth) would have the occasion to test our abilities on a 'fresh' jetty.

The rains had, meanwhile, picked up a bit and a fair onshore wind had also started blowing. Even as we started aligning ourselves with the lay of the jetty (with various memorised situations from seamanship manuals flashing inside my brain), we realised that the manoeuvres could get a bit tricky. The wind was pushing us a lot more onto the fast approaching berth jetty, and the rain of course could make things less reactive for the Anchor and Cable Party if they had to drop anchor in an emergency.

The Navigator, meanwhile, was watching from his compass binnacle like a hawk, keeping a very close watch on bearing changes[1]. About two-ship length away, and he softly advised slowing down, to take the way off the frigate. I was not convinced, and keeping full faith in the hugely powerful GTs (these allow extreme manoeuvres from full speed to a dead stop if it came to that), ordered maintenance of the same speed.

But lo and behold, as we closed on, I realised the Navigator was right (most seasoned pilots invariably always are!). Sensing the intuitive risk of some damage or scraping of the ship's side as we started paralleling out[2], I finally voiced the orders for slowing down the lumbering ship, which now seemed to have a mind of her own. Simultaneously, I jumped from my chair and dashed towards the Port Bridge Wing (minus rain gear) to better con the ship. Even as the ship's

1. The change in bearing of various shore navigation marks are very important for the Bridge to approach and secure the ship alongside.
2. A Naval ship approaches the jetty or another ship at an angle and then straightens or parallels out to have a precise berth.

astern motion kicked in, I did the inevitable (which gravity I realised only later on), I raised both hands ahead as if to push against the jetty side walls in a bid to give our ship more time to slide slowly and smoothly alongside, which she did with aplomb.

As the EXO guided the latter part of getting the ship's hawsers tied up onto the jetty bollards, I exchanged a slightly sheepish glance with the Navigator, who, unsurprisingly, was his usual calm and impassive self.

As we shared a glass of beer at my cabin after the ship was fully secured, I extolled the Navigator's keen and truly professional eye and advice.

"But Sir, all this was also due to your will and push", said he, with a twinkle in his eyes.

It made me realise then that I was now truly one with the graceful loyalty of the magnificent Ship!

□

GLOSSARY

Academy Term: A typical duration of around five months. A three-year Academy tenure has six terms.

Action Stations: The crew of Naval ships and submarines attain this status during imminent attack or defence against enemy forces, or even during specialist evolutions like carrying out replenishment at sea.

Active Mode: This mode of underwater operation in water involves use of active echo location wherein the sonar transmits sound waves of specific frequency, to locate or home onto targets. It can be tactically used by a submarine or fired torpedo.

Anchor and Cable Party: A group of sailors supervised by the Gunnery Officer, in the Forecastle of a ship. They are responsible for letting go the anchor and required cable length, upon orders from Bridge.

Attack Periscope: A periscope normally only used during tracking and attack on targets by submarines. May be used by the Captain during planing to periscope depth.

Astern: To move or propel in a backward direction, for a ship or submarine

ASWO: A qualified officer on a Naval ship or submarine, responsible for all operations involving underwater weapon and sensore. He can also supervise diving crew operations in case a Diving cadre officer is not separately appointed on-board the vessel.

Ballast: Weights installed for stability on a marine vessel. It could also refer to added sea water in specific tanks on a submarine to achieve diving into the ocean depths.

Basic Submarines Course: A comprehensive Training Course for all budding submariners.

Blind Pilotage: The process of navigating in Pilotage-waters during low visibility conditions. Primary sensor used is the Navigation Radar.

Binnacle: The structure which consists of a stand housing the main compass installed on gimbals in a ship's Bridge. This could be used for navigating in Pilotage-waters as well as various exercise manoeuvres at sea.

Boat: Apart from normal usage, it can also refer to a submarine (short for the dreaded U-boats of WW2)

Bollard: Fittings on a ship, a submarine or a jetty/pier for tying up berthing hawsers or any wire ropes

'Bottle': A reprimand in Navy terminology is indicated as getting a bottle.

Bridge: The primary control centre on a Naval ship, or in the sail of a submarine (while it is on surface). The Captain normally operates from this post while at sea.

Bridge Wings: The passages on both port and starboard sides outside an enclosed Bridge on a naval ship.

Bulkhead Door: Any door leading to the bulkhead infrastructure of a ship. Bulkhead refers to the walls inside a ship or submarine.

BZ: It stands for 'Bravo zulu' in Naval lingo. Indicates a pat on the back for a job very well done.

Captain's Chair: A chair installed in the Naval ship's Bridge, specifically only for the Captain of the vessel

Captain's Standing Orders: This is a document which lays down important Standard Operating Procedures, and various Do's and Dont's for officers who get appointed on-

board a Naval ship or submarine.

Casing: The upper walking deck on a submarine.

Call Sign: Each Naval ship or submarine has its unique call sign used during communications with shore authorities or between friendly Naval units.

Cable: A unit of length 10 cables make up one sea nautical mile (around 1.8 km on land).

Catwalk: The passageways on either sides on the main walking deck of a ship.

CDO: Clearance Diving Officer. They form the mainstay of the Diving branch along with the ship's divers. CDOs carry out diving operations to deeper depths, and could be trained in covert underwater operations against enemy units.

Chief Petty Officer (CPO): Ranked above the Petty Officer-in-Charge, these sailors could be supervising a group of junior sailors of various ratings.

Check Dive: After a Long Refit (from six months duration onwards), a submarine needs to undergo an intial controlled dive, to check watertightness of all on-board systems.

Choke Point Patrols: Submarines are also sometimes used for patrolling in restricted waters near enemy waters, which could constrict their ships' movements.

C-in-C: The Commander-in-Chief of a Naval Command HQ.

CO: Short for Commanding Officer.

Control Room: The main control post in a submarine for steering, diving/surfacing, navigation, Fire Control System (FCS) operations, etc.

Commander: A mid-level Naval rank for officers. The EXO of a capital Naval ship can also be referred to as the Ship's Commander.

CIC (Combat Information Centre): Some submarines have an additional compartment for watching on various sensors like ESM, sonar, radar etc.

Coxswain: The Naval sailor or Officer- in-Charge of a boat, especially its navigation and steering. It also refers to the head of the seamen department responsible to the EXO of a Naval submarine.

Commodore: A senior level officer rank in the Navy.

'Dolphin' badge: The coveted badge of submariners worldwide. It indicates that the wearer is a qualified submariner. Awarded after passing a qualification Board assessment consequent to a long Submarine School training, Escape Training and practical hands on visits to submarines.

Dived Watch-keeping Ticket: A submarine branch officer needs to be assessed and qualify for this Certificate before undertaking independent watches on a dived submarine.

Depth Charge: These are launched explosives, used against submarines by Naval ships, helicopters or patrol aircraft.

Degaussing: This is an evolution to reduce the magnetic signature of a submarine.

Detachment: Smaller independent shore units set up mostly along the coasts, by the Navy.

Damage Control (DC): The system organisation and processes to contain and repair any damages due to battle attacks, water ingress, etc., to a Naval ship or submarine. Every unit has an earmarked DC party trained in handling any such emergency.

Defaulter: A Naval crew sailor who is charged with an act of indiscipline.

Dry Dock: A manmade structure within a dockyard, where ships and submarines are placed using chocks or beams, during refit and repairs of these vessels.

Directorate: The Naval HQ is divided into multiple Directorates which are the nodal offices responsible for various arms, and services of the Navy, e.g., Directorate of Submarine

Operations, Directorate of Victuals and Clothing etc.

Divisions: A ceremonial parade in specified uniform generally conducted on occasions like Independence Day, visit of political VIPs, very senior Naval authorities, or even on regular basis parade inspection by COs of naval unit (afloat or ashore).

ESM: Electronic Support Measures, which include watch on enemy radar frequencies for early warning of incoming air strikes, missile launches, or other ships' gunnery fire control radars etc.

Enterprise: A popular light two-crewed sailing boat used for recreational purpose or competitive racing.

EWO: Electronic Warfare Officer, responsible for undertaking all Electronic Warfare measures on-board a Naval ship.

Executive Officer (EXO): Second-in-command of a Naval submarine or ship. Also referred to as No. 2 by the Captain.

ETA: Expected time of arrival.

Escape Drills: All submariners need to qualify in these drills to escape from a sunk submarine, using a rubberised fully body wet suit and closed cycle breathing apparatus.

EO: The Officer who heads the Engineering department of a Naval ship or a submarine.

Forecastle: The forward (pointing ahead) section of a marine vessel.

Galley: Navy term for kitchen. Also the source of the phrase 'galley gossip'.

Gemini: A rubber dinghy fitted with an Outboard Motor, used mainly by Ship's divers. Fully portable when deflated.

Gangway: The brow or plank, which is used to traverse from a jetty or pier to the upper deck of a ship or a submarine. It can be a basic wooden plank or a manufactured one made of metal and with hand railings.

Hatch: A round opening (mostly for vertical transit) leading from one deck to another in a ship or a submarine.

Heads: Navy term for the toilets on-board a ship or a submarine.

Hawser: The berthing ropes for a ship or a submarine, made of nylon or polypropylene.

HELO Deck: A helicopter pad located in the stern of the ship. It incorporates equipment, hangars, etc., for the helicopter operations.

International Fleet Review: A periodic review by the President, of ships, submarines and aircraft of own and diverse foreign guest Navies.

Jacob's ladder: A flexible ladder made of wire rope and wood/ metal steps. Used to climb up sides of a ship, or lower onto a smaller vessel from a big ship.

JOM: Junior Officers Mess. Generally used for lodging of Sub Lts. borne for watch-keeping and sometimes also used by Midshipmen on Naval ships.

Letting go: To unberth involving taking out the hawser eye from a bollard, so the ship or submarine is unattached to the jetty or pier and free to maneouvre on its own.

Liberty: Naval ships allow sailors or trainee officer cadets to leave ship for personal or other reasons of shore leave, etc., normally at the end of the working day.

Lieutenant (Lt): The second rank for a Naval officer.

LO: The Electrial Officer who heads the Electrical department of a Naval ship or a submarine.

Log: The mechanism that allows measurement and indication of the speed of a ship or a submarine.

Lookout: Every ship or submarine has sailor staff posted as lookouts on the Bridge. They are entrusted to scan the vastness of the sea around the vessel to detect and report other shipping traffic, boats, sailing vessels, etc.

LtCdr: An officer rank in the Navy, attained after around nine years of service.

Master-Chief-At-Arms: The head of the Regulating / Provost Department sailors on a Naval afloat or a shore unit.

'Manning': Every post is manned physically by a Naval crew member on a ship or a submarine.

Middle watch: The watch, typically from 12 am till 4 am on-board a ship. Also sometimes referred to as the 'graveyard watch'.

Magpie: The term used for the outer edges of the target board used during small arms firing practices.

MCGI: Master Chief Gunnery Instructor, responsible to the Gunnery Officer during gunnery or missile shooting exercises, and also for imparting drill and parade training for sailors and Midshipmen .

MOD: Midshipman of the Day. He/she assists the OOD and Assistant OOD.

Matching bearings: A last step in a submarine's attack manoeuvres, prior to firing a torpedo.

Main Switch Board (MSB): Every Naval ship and submarine has the MSB, from where all propulsion and lighting power and auxiliary systems are operated and controlled.

Morse Code: The traditional code language used by vessels at sea for communication. Nowadays most Navies have replaced this with more modern systems.

MOW (Midshipman of the Watch): Assists the OOW in the Bridge of a Naval ship.

Navigation Lights: Every Naval vessel has a specific configuration of lights used during dark hours or low visibility at sea.

Navigator/Navigating Officer/'Pilot': The right hand man of the Captain of a ship or a submarine at sea. He/she is responsible for virtually all kinds of operations of the ship, as

well as guiding and advising the Captain on the Bridge during entering or leaving any harbour.

OOD: Officer of the Day who is responsible for the Naval ship or submarine for a 24-hour period. He is the representative of the Captain of the Ship.

'One-eyed Lady': Connotation for a periscope (since most submarines of particular classes had periscopes which allow only a single eye lens for use).

'Old Man': The common Naval usage for the Captain of a Naval unit.

OIC: Officer-in-Charge, who commands smaller Naval shore units or detachments.

OJT: On job training on a ship or a submarine, for learning about operating , repair and rectification of various systems and sensors.

Observer: Typically, naval multi-role bigger helicopters and LRMP aircraft have an officer of Observer cadre, who is responsible for collating and analysing information from diverse sensors like ESM, sonar, etc. They can advise the HELO Pilot in various tactical manoeuvres and weapon use.

OBM: Outboard Motor used on various small craft like Gemini, small patrol boats, etc.

OEM: Original equipment manufacturer.

OOW: Officer of the Watch. He/she is responsible for all navigational safety and operational manoeuvres of a ship or a submarine during a four hours or three hours watch on a Naval ship or a submarine respectively.

Ops Room: A command and control centre on a Naval ship from where the Captain can conduct various evolutions like gunnery missile attacks, tactical manoeuvring, etc.

PCO Course: Principal Control Officers Course for Submarine arm Executive branch officers, for qualifying to undertake the responsibility and appointment as Executive

Officer of a Naval submarine.

PCT: Pre-commissioning training for appointments on Naval ships, or conversion to a different class of submarines.

PCT-OJT Board: The in-house Board, which assesses officers after the PCT and a specific duration of OJT.

Petty Officer In-Charge: An important working and supervising level for sailor crew of a Naval unit.

Pontoon: The rubber buffer protectors between two ships or submarines when berthed in harbour. They keep the respective vessels sides away from each other, especially the underwater appendages.

Practice Torpedo Firings: Ships, submarines and naval HELOs undertake such exercises at sea using torpedoes with no warheads.

Part of Ship: Each section of a Naval ship forms part of a ship like Forecastle, Quarterdeck, etc.

Passive Mode: This mode of underwater operation in water involves using passive sonar in sound reception mode only. Can be tactically used by a submarine or a fired torpedo, or dunked sonar of ASW helo, or sonobuoys.

'Pips': Refers to the shoulder rank tabs of Naval officers.

Punkah louvers: A typical reference to outlets for cool air on a Naval ship or submarine.

Quarterdeck: The raised deck at the stern section of a marine vessel. Traditionally the Naval ship's Ensign Flag is flown at the aft most tip of the Quarterdeck.

Refit: The periodic or as required basis repair and overhaul of systems, machinery and hull work for a Naval ship or a submarine.

Radar Index Error: The error inherent in the ranges of objects and vessels indicated by marine radars.

Requestmen: A formal periodic procedure conducted by

the EXO for grant of promotions, good conduct awards, etc., to sailors of a Naval unit.

Submarine Board: Board conducted to assess and qualify officers as 'Dolphin' badge holders, after the Basic Submarine Course and on-board OJT.

Surface Watch-keeping Ticket: A Submarine branch officer or a Naval ship officer has to be assessed and qualify for this Certificate before carrying out independent watches at sea.

Sub-Lieutenant: The first rank for officers on commissioning into the Navy.

Sub-Lieutenant Technical Courses: A nearly yearlong course for Sub Lts. of the Executive branch, to prepare them for appointments on-board Naval afloat units.

Snorting: State of a diesel-electric submarine while it is charging its batteries.

Search Periscope: The main periscope used on-board a submarine, used for surveillance to detect other vessels on sea surface or air contacts.

Semaphore: A code using a set of hand flags, for visual communication between Naval marine units at sea.

Singling Up: Normally berthing hawsers are doubled up for firm securing of a Naval ship or a submarine. During letting-go process, they are singled upon Bridge orders.

Steward: A Naval sailor responsible for serving food and drinks in a Wardroom. He can also assist the Cook in the galley for various jobs.

Shore Office: A submarine's personnel typically used a Shore Office for office and staff work, when in harbour.

'Snotty': Old naval term for Midshipman.

SCO: Signal Communications Officer on a ship or a submarine.

Ship's Duty Watch: Each naval ship and submarine

necessarily has such a team of personnel responsible to the OOD. They need to undertake firefighting drills, work various machinery in harbour, receive rations or other items, during off hours.

SSE: Submerged signal ejector. This is a projectile discharged through a tube from a submarine, essentially to indicate its position during exercises with ships. The SSE can give off various-coloured smoke and a flare.

Torpedo: The main tactical weapon for a submarine. The warhead has sufficient explosive power to sink a large capital ship.

'Trick': A common Naval usage for a watch at sea.

Transducer: The basic sensor unit for a sonar of a Naval ship, submarine, dunking helo or sonobuoy deployed by Naval LRMP aircraft.

Trot: The sailor manning the point where the gangway touches a submarine's upper deck. He is responsible for security from entry of any unauthorised person, registering names of any extra personnel or items entering on-board, paying of ceremonial salutes or pipes for senior officials , as a communication hand to attend to any queries from personnel inside the submarine, lookout for any dangerous underwater devices or personnel which could harm the vessel, etc.

Upper Lid: This is a steel vacuum sealed hatch, which is shut off prior to diving a submarine

Watch: Tenure of a duty on-board Naval ships and submarines at sea.

Watch-keeping Officer: Officers of rank of Sub Lt./Lt. get appointed on ships and submarines for doing independent watches at sea.

Wardroom: This is the dining-cum-entertainment space on a ship, a submarine or a shore messing facility for Naval officers.

Weapons Officer/Torpedo Officer: An officer who is responsible to the Captain of a submarine, for efficient and effective operations of the Weapons department (including torpedoes, missiles, mines, etc.).

Whaler: A standard wooden boat used by crew of naval ships for surviving at sea from a sunk ship, retrieving anybody falling overboard, or for racing competitions between Fleet ships. It can be used with oars or sails.

WTO: Wireless Telegraph Office, wherein all communication operations are undertaken on a Naval ship.

Warping: Term used for manoeuvring a ship or a submarine using only her hawsers.